You Killed my Brother

BOOK 1 OF THE CULTURES COLLIDE SERIES

KEITH ROMMEL

MILFORD
HOUSE

an imprint of Sunbury Press, Inc.
Mechanicsburg, PA USA

MILFORD
HOUSE

an imprint of Sunbury Press, Inc.
Mechanicsburg, PA USA

For information about special discounts for bulk purchases, please contact Sunbury Press Orders Dept. at (855) 338-8359 or orders@sunburypress.com.

To request one of our authors for speaking engagements or book signings, please contact Sunbury Press Publicity Dept. at publicity@sunburypress.com.

FIRST MILFORD HOUSE PRESS EDITION: September 2025

Set in Adobe Garamond Pro | Interior design by Crystal Devine | Cover design by Lawrence Knorr | Edited by Amanda Shrawder.

Publisher's Cataloging-in-Publication Data
Names: Rommel, Keith, author.
Title: You killed my brother / Keith Rommel.
Description: First trade paperback edition. | Mechanicsburg, PA : Milford House Press, 2025.
Summary: When a jury hands out a lenient sentence, the protagonist sets out to avenge his family's suffering. But what he forgets in his rage is that for every action, there is a reaction.
Identifiers: ISBN 979-8-88819-406-5 (softcover).
Subjects: FICTION / Horror | FICTION / Thrillers / Crime.

Designed in the USA
0 1 1 2 3 5 8 13 21 34 55

For the Love of Books!

To God and the mysteries of this life.

Wonder about your future only briefly as you are here now.
Live your life and love others without limitations.
Tomorrow may never come.

Other books by
KEITH ROMMEL

THE CURSED MAN

THE LURKING MAN

THE SINFUL MAN

THE SILENT WOMAN

among the people

chapter 1

IF MURDER WERE legal, there would be dozens of bodies left in Jennifer's wake.

"Damn it," she whispered, and heaved a sigh. She stared at the caravan of cars that inched forward and squeezed the steering wheel. They went on as far as the eye could see, hardly moving. She rested her elbow on the armrest and pushed taut fingers through her hair.

"Mom?"

Jennifer looked into the rearview mirror and both Emily and Hannah stared back.

"Yes?" Jennifer said with the most patient voice she could muster.

"You shouldn't say words like that mommy," Emily said.

"You're right, I shouldn't. I'm sorry."

"Do you think we're going to be late, is that why you're mad?" Emily said.

The clock on the car radio read 4:00.

"I hope not," Jennifer said, but deep down inside she didn't think their tardiness was avoidable. She clamped her eyes shut and tried to ignore a deep pain that pulsed and hid tactfully behind her eyes.

"Are you not feeling well, mommy?" Hannah said.

"Mommy's fine," she said. "I am just worried that we are going to be late and that will make me and your daddy late for the event."

"It's okay," Hannah said and looked out the side window. "You shouldn't worry so much. Daddy is the star and they can't do anything without him."

Jennifer laughed. "I suppose you're right." She watched as a car rode the shoulder all the way to the next exit.

"Mommy, you should follow him," Emily said, and pointed at the car that Jennifer watched. "He's going fast!"

"I . . ." Jennifer thought to protest the suggestion, but knew it was the only way. The risk of getting a ticket was worth the time she could save. She cut the wheel hard right and stepped on the gas. The powerful car raced up the shoulder and approached another long line of cars that led to a blinking traffic light. She pressed the brake pedal hard and stopped the car just short of the vehicle in front of her. The force of the abrupt halt pushed everyone forward in their seats and snapped them back.

"I'm sorry," Jennifer said. "I didn't mean to do that."

"You don't think daddy will leave without you, do you?" Hannah said, her eyes wide with the question.

"No, I don't suppose he would."

The vehicles ahead of her managed to merge their way into traffic quicker than she anticipated.

"He loves you too much to do that," Hannah said. "He tells you that all the time."

"You are very smart." Jennifer smiled.

She had tried to organize the events of this day in advance and believed she had given herself plenty of time to complete her tasks and ready the children before her husband arrived home. She had intended to have everyone ready for the evening's event prior to the babysitter's arrival. That way there would be no stress and the perfect tone would be set for the night.

"Something going perfectly, imagine that . . ." she whispered and chuckled at the thought.

"Mommy, what did you say?" Emily said.

"Nothing, honey. I'm just talking to myself."

Her day had started off with a routine checkup at the dentist's office. From there she had gone directly to the woman's health clinic because she hadn't been feeling well the last few weeks and her appetite had grown substantially.

"I just knew it," she said, and rubbed her belly.

She couldn't wait to share the news with her husband, Rainer, but had already decided that she would wait until tomorrow to do that. This was his day and he deserved the attention without anything taking away from it. He worked hard and gave so much of himself to everyone.

Jennifer inched the car to the blinking light and she looked left and then to the right. A steady flow of cars came from both directions.

"Mommy?"

Jennifer looked in the rearview mirror. Emily had unbuckled her harness and had climbed out of her booster seat. She was standing between the driver and passenger seats.

"Emily!" Jennifer said, and quickly turned and faced her daughter. "Get back in your seat!"

"But mom!"

"Now!"

"But . . ."

"No buts, Emily. Do what I'm telling you to. Do it right now!"

Jennifer put the car in park and grabbed Emily by the arm and forced her into her seat.

"I've told you never to do this!"

"You hurt my arm!"

"It's better than you going flying through the windshield! I told you getting out of your seat is dangerous and you can get hurt!"

Emily's face reddened and her eyes welled with tears. Her bottom lip curled and her expression contorted into something horrible.

"You hurt me mom!"

"Why can't you stay in your seat like your sister?"

Honk.

"Why?" Jennifer said, her frustration turning to anger.

Emily looked at her twin sister and she was buckled in her seat. She looked at her mother with a blank stare. She rubbed her arm.

"Do you want a policeman to come and take you away from me?"

Emily shook her head and began to pout. "Uncle Glenn wouldn't do that to me."

"He would if he found out what you were doing."

Honk.

"Stop beeping your damn horn!" Jennifer yelled, staring out the back window.

Emily folded her arms across her chest. "No, he wouldn't!"

"Yes, he would."

Emily kicked the back of her mother's seat. "And I said he wouldn't!"

Honk.

3

Jennifer glared at her daughter. "Don't you dare talk back to your mother like that. I'll take the television away from you for a week."

"I don't care!"

Jennifer swiped an open hand across Emily's cheek.

A boiling wail erupted from Emily. Hannah looked at her sister and she started to cry. A chorus of shouts filled the vehicle and brought Jennifer's headache to a whole new level.

"I'm telling daddy you hit me!"

"And I'm not going to tell you again. Don't you dare get out of that seat!"

Jennifer buckled her in and sharply turned her attention to Hannah. "And you have nothing to be crying about."

Jennifer faced forward and stomped the gas pedal and the car lurched into the middle of the intersection. In a moment of clarity, Jennifer noticed a bluish colored car skidding towards her and she screamed. It approached at a speed and angle that seemed impossible to avoid.

RUTH DRUMMED HER fingers on the steering wheel of the 1978 Chevy Nova. She rocked back and forth to the distorted rhythm of a punk rock band blaring from the speakers. A lit cigarette hung loosely between her lips and its long ash end threatened to break away.

"You thankless bastard," she said and bit back at the surging anger. She turned the radio up louder.

Fast food wrappers, empty beer cans and dirty clothes were strewn about the floor, passenger, and back seat of the vehicle.

"Brick," she said through clenched teeth. Bad thoughts continued to come and they crinkled her brows. "The moment I see you, you're going to get the biggest smack of your life."

Ruth tried to roll down the window, but the frigid conditions outside held it closed. She applied pressure to the window crank and the frozen seal let go with a pop. Despite the subzero temperature outside, she lowered the window halfway.

"No, first I'm going to tell him what an asshole he is, and then I'll hit him."

Although both ideas sounded great when she played them out in her mind, she knew neither would happen so she submitted to her anger.

"You're an insensitive bastard. Brick the dick."

She knew she was going to melt when she saw him and jump into his arms. The strength in his hug would be enough to make her forget. Knowing he was out of prison and would be around every day was enough to help her forget any bad he might have done.

"And what does it really matter anyway?"

She looked at her eyes in the rearview mirror and they were bright red. "That was some good shit," she said and laughed. "I've got to remember to have Alvaro get me more of that."

A shiver rocked her body.

"Damn it."

The bite of the frigid air was fierce. A foggy haze started to form on the window. She bunched her sleeve in her hand and mopped the glass while she searched the dashboard for the heat control.

"Man, this cold is awful!"

Her teeth chattered and she rolled the window up. She placed her numb fingers close to the heat vents and the cigarette dropped its ashen end.

"Damn, that feels good," she said, switching her hands back and forth in front of the vent, steering with one, and warming the other.

Something stung her thigh, demanding her immediate attention. She swiped a hand across her leg and brushed away the cigarette ash that burned her skin.

"You son of a bitch!"

The fiery sensation lingered like the prick from a needle. She clenched her teeth and pounded her fist off of the dashboard.

She looked at the small burn hole in her jeans. "Great. Now my buzz is gone and my only good pair of pants are ruined."

At that moment, she caught a glimpse of something hurrying in front of her car and she jerked the wheel left. White-knuckled fingers held on tight as the vehicle went into a skid.

WHEN JENNIFER STARTED to scream, she clamped her eyes shut and braced herself for impact. She had allowed her emotions to get the better of her and she'd lashed out at her own child and didn't look before she applied pressure to the gas pedal. She catapulted herself, her children and unborn child into the waiting arms of tragedy.

What kind of mother would do something like that?

Her concept of time left her, and the screams of her frightened children were drowned out by the haunting screech of an approaching vehicle that skidded and turned at an awkward angle.

Then as quickly as the sound of chaos erupted around her, everything suddenly fell silent. It was awful, this silence, and it begged attention. Jennifer hesitated, but found the courage to open her eyes.

The engine knocked, puked a thick black plume of smoke, and then stalled. The radio cut out and the heat died. Having looked over her shoulder to peer out the rear window, Ruth saw the white car that was responsible for nearly killing her.

Her adrenaline began to race and she had to know what the driver of the other vehicle was doing.

Ruth pulled the lever but the door held closed. "If they were on their phone, I'm going to break it over their head."

She threw a shoulder into it and forced it open, but only slightly. Hitting the door a second time, though stubborn, it gave way and opened fully with a creak.

"What the hell is wrong with you?" Ruth said. The thick lingering cloud of burnt rubber and gray blue exhaust masked the occupants of the white car.

Ruth strutted towards the car and a million different thoughts of what she might do when she came nose to nose with the driver raced through her mind. Man or woman, it didn't matter. One thing she decided was that slap she had been saving for Brick was going to be used on the moron that operated that white car instead.

Once she came within a few feet of the vehicle, she pointed and laughed at the petite woman latched onto the steering wheel. Her fear was obvious, and she appeared as though she had spent too many hours in a tanning bed. The dead animal she had snug around her neck and the fancy car she drove were an insult to the working class.

"Maybe you should have purchased some driving lessons instead of worrying about all of the crap you surround yourself with. No one cares how rich you are, you moron!"

Ruth slapped the window to gain the woman's attention. "Hey, I'm talking to you! What in the hell is wrong with you? Are you blind or something?"

The tan-faced woman looked at her with a distant, unconcerned look. Her children were crying and they both had rotten faces covered with snot and tears.

Ruth pounded the window a second time and the tan-faced woman mouthed the words *I'm sorry*. The insincere gesture only intensified Ruth's anger and she pounded on the hood of the car.

"You know what, you little bitch, why don't you get out of the car so I can give you what you deserve for almost killing me!"

Ruth pulled on the door handle and it was locked.

The tan-face woman turned to calm her children and seemed hardly concerned by Ruth's outbursts.

"You think you can ignore me?" Ruth said.

She backed up three steps and hopped twice before she planted her foot on the front quarter panel of the car. In front of the wheel, the metal bent inwards and the vehicle rocked from the force of the blow.

Ruth laughed as she inspected the damage her kick had left behind. She pointed at the dent and turned her attention to the driver. "You see? That's just what you deserve! Now get out of the car and do something about it!"

The petite woman rolled down the window a crack and said something that was inaudible to Ruth. It was drowned out by the swooping wind and the howls that came from the children.

"What?" Ruth said and moved her ear to the window.

Jumbled shouts and chaos within the car continued to drown out the woman's voice but the way her mouth moved with the accentuated creases in her skin reminded Ruth of an old leather baseball mitt that needed to be oiled. It was annoying and her fist would do it some good.

The kids continued to scream and carry on and Ruth laughed knowing she was able to return the favor of ruining someone's day.

"Hey," Ruth said, her stern focus on the children. "Shut the hell up, you spoiled little shits!"

The words scared the children into silence.

"There you go," Ruth said and looked at Jennifer. "Now you. Is there something wrong with you? Are you trying to kill someone?"

"They're just kids," tan-face said, and her curt response turned Ruth's lips upwards into a satisfied grin.

"Why don't you get out of your car and do something about it?"

"I said I was sorry. What happened was an honest mistake. Now please just leave us alone."

Ruth's shoulders slumped and she shook her head. "Just when I thought things were going to get interesting, you go and say something as weak as that. It was an accident, my ass!" Ruth said, and drove her finger into the window. "You were probably on your damn cell phone booking your next tanning session and you nearly killed me in the process."

A large man wrapped in an apron stained with blood stepped off the curb and stole Ruth's attention. She swung around to face him and reached her hand inside her coat. She paused, her eyes wide, filled with warning. "You should mind your own business, fat man, and walk away."

The meat man raised his hands in surrender and took a few steps away. "Take it easy. I don't want any trouble. I'm just making sure everyone's okay and this doesn't get out of control."

"Everyone is fine and this ain't none of your damn business," Ruth said.

Tan-face knocked on her window and showed Ruth her cell phone. "You should leave now because I'm calling the police."

"And if I wanted, you'd be dead before they even got here," Ruth said with fire in her eyes. "Rich assholes like you think they own the damn world."

She pulled her hand out of her pocket and made it into a gun. She aimed it at tan-face and pushed her thumb down.

"Bang, you're dead. It would be that simple."

She started to walk away.

"No," Ruth said, paused, and then turned around and kicked a second dent into the quarter panel.

Satisfied that they were even now, she walked back to her car with a confident swagger. She reached inside her car for a lighter and looked back at the white car. Lighting the cigarette, she took a deep drag and stared at tan-face for a few moments. She showed her the middle finger and laughed merrily when the woman looked away.

Sitting inside her car, she twisted the key in the ignition and the machine whined. The tired old engine sputtered to life and belched a thick cloud of gray smoke that added to the already murky air. Ruth threw the car into drive and stomped the gas pedal and sang along to a song filled with hate and aggression.

EDDIE TREMBLED AT the sound of skidding tires and braced himself for the violent sound of impact. After a few tense moments, he sighed in relief. Thankful that he wouldn't be pulling bloody people out of their twisted, collapsed cars and having to offer them what little assistance he could until the paramedics came, he sighed again.

His two year service to his country in Iraq taught him basic skills to keep the wounded alive and aware long enough until the field doctor came. The violence of war and the memories woke him on many nights throughout the years and never seemed to dull. Each and every person that had been hurt on that corner over the years reminded him of days he would rather forget. Pain-filled faces and pleading eyes haunted him every night and this location only added to his closet full of ghosts.

Eddie looked Heavenward. "Thank you Lord I wasn't slicing meat," he said.

Eddie wiped his hands on his apron and mindlessly grabbed a foam plate off the countertop. He approached the large storefront window and glanced outside. A thick haze clouded the air and to his relief he didn't see any mangled vehicles or bodies strewn about.

On his way out the door, he reminded himself he was going through this at least twice a week. Why would a nonfunctioning traffic light remain broken for so long—especially one that was right off of a major parkway? How many people would have to get injured or even die before they finally did something about it?

He watched dumbfounded as a plump young woman ran around wildly. She shouted obscenities, made threats and kicked massive dents into the side of a white car. Whatever was going on looked as though it was getting out of hand, and he knew he needed to intervene before someone got hurt. He stepped into the street, and despite his massive size, he was uneasy about the young woman's crazy behavior.

JENNIFER STARED AT Ruth as she walked away. Disbelief that some-one so young could be so intensely mean and unforgiving held her jaw agape. The twins continued to whimper in their fear, and she looked at them in hopes of being able to calm them.

"It's okay now. The bad woman is going away."

A knock on the side window startled Jennifer and she responded with a screech. She tried to scoot to the passenger seat but the belt she wore kept her in place. The children started to scream again and their shouts were ear piercing.

Worried that the girl had returned to follow through with her threats, she looked at an overweight man that wore a bloody apron and was motioning for her to roll down her window. In light of recent events, she didn't consider it. She threw the car into drive and began to roll out of the intersection.

The overweight man jogged next to her car and struggled to keep up. He pressed a foam plate with sloppy handwriting on it to the window and knocked again. "Come on lady," he said. "I can't keep this up much longer. I just want to give you the license plate number to that girl's car."

Jennifer looked at the writing and slowed her car to a stop. She rolled her window down a crack and accepted the information with a smile filled with shame. "I'm sorry," she said, and checked her rearview mirror. "But I didn't know if you were with her."

"If I was, then this would have been a great way for me to gain your trust. No doubt about it, I'd have you where I wanted you. But I'm not." He pointed at his store. "I own the butcher shop," he said, and struggled to catch his breath. "Besides, I don't normally walk around town like this." He tugged on his apron and smiled. "People might think I'm a little crazy."

Jennifer returned the smile and placed the foam plate into the glove box. "Thank you for your trouble."

"Don't mention it," he said. "My name is Eddie DePina. If you need a witness statement or something, I have no problem doing that for you. You know where to find me."

"Thank you, that is very kind of you," Jennifer said, and realized the children had quieted and her hands had stopped shaking. She smiled knowing there were still some kind people left in the world. And luckily for her, this one just happened to be close by when she needed him most.

"If you would like to come into my shop, I can call the police for you if that makes you feel any safer?" Eddie looked down the street both ways. "I'm sure she couldn't have gotten too far."

"Thank you, but I'm going to have to decline."

"You have a pretty big dent in your car and you seem pretty shook up by what just happened. Are you sure?"

"Yes, I'm sure. I have somewhere to go and I'm already late. Did you know who she was?"

Eddie shook his head. "She's a local street thug. I have seen her here and there and I think she runs with a gang or something. Obviously they have nothing better to do than try and scare people."

"I don't trust that prick," Ruth said, and turned down the first side street she found and doubled back. She made sure she was far enough away so that she wouldn't be seen. Pulling the car to the curb, she stalled the engine. Her gaze settled on the fat man. She was positive that he wasn't going to heed her warning and mind his own business. And once he crossed that line from stupid to disrespectful, she would send him a message he would never forget.

As if on cue, she observed the fat man scrutinize the roads on which she had departed and soon after, he approached the white car that nearly rammed her. She wasn't expecting anything less out of him because she remembered him and how he couldn't keep his nose out of other people's business.

The memory was from a time when Brick and Beto got along. From a time she wished would never have ended.

She laughed at the memory and enjoyed it with a smile.

Before the group had a name they hung out at the local high school. They gathered on the dark side of the bleachers that surrounded the football field. They drank beer, smoked a little weed and exchanged stories about what mischief they caused. But on one particular night when the beer began to run low, even though they couldn't come up with five dollars combined, her, Brick and Beto volunteered to go on a beer run and they promised everyone they would return with more alcohol before their buzz started to wear off.

Almost an entire hour had passed before they were able to reunite with the group. Their foreheads were sweaty and they panted from climbing fences, hiding in dark places, and sprinting from cover to cover. When Brick finally caught his breath, he had explained why they were gone for so long and why they had returned empty handed.

"So I'm in the back of Cono's deli stuffing beers into my coat," Brick had said. "I'm loading the sleeves, stuffing the inside pockets, just putting crap anywhere I could fit it. When I couldn't fit anymore, I zipped my jacket up to my neck while Beto and Ruth tried to distract that crazy old man that own the place."

"His name is Cono," Macho said.

Macho was Brick's older brother, the founder and leader of the gang.

"That's right, crazy Cono," Brick said. "Man that guy is out there." He rolled his eyes.

Everyone agreed.

"Anyway, they had me laughing when they were shaming crazy Cono, telling him he was trying to sell them expired milk on purpose and that they had a baby at home. That distraction was enough, but for some reason they didn't think so."

Brick spat and wiped the sweat from his forehead.

"We were trying to get him away from the front door," Ruth said.

"By bringing him to the section I was loading up in?"

"We wanted to make sure you had a clear path to the door," Beto said.

"Anyways, when they walked him down the aisle, I simply walked past them with hardly a problem."

"You see?" Ruth said.

"The bottles in my jacket made all sorts of clanking sounds and I was nervous as hell, but crazy Cono didn't even look at me. When I got to the door, the fat butcher dude from next door comes into the store, waving a fifty-dollar bill over his head and shouting how he needed change."

Ruth waddled and waved her hands over her head like a monkey. She imitated the fat guy and the group of kids laughed at her antics.

"No way," Macho said. "That guy is a big dude. When you saw him did you about crap yourself or what?"

Brick paused and puffed his chest. "Me?" He exhaled. "Yeah, a little."

The group roared in laughter.

"But hold on, the story gets even better," Brick said. "So the fat guy walked right into me like I wasn't even there. I bounced off of him and a beer rolled out of my jacket and smashed on the floor between us. I'm standing there now, thinking like, 'Oh shit, what the hell should I do?' and I go to run. The guy reaches for me and I swear to God his arm was like five feet long and his hand was as big as a catcher's mitt, because he caught me by my jacket and yanked me backwards like I was a rag doll. I fell to the floor and beer bottles flew everywhere, smashing all around me like bombs being dropped out of an airplane. I went to get up and he stomped down on my chest, forcing the air out of my lungs. I was pinned to the ground and gasping for air. I swear, I thought I was going to die."

Macho shook his head. "There wasn't any fat man and there wasn't any attempt at nabbing us some beers. You all are a bunch of pussies."

"No man, I'm serious," Brick said, and looked at Beto for confirmation. "Right, man?"

All eyes shifted to Beto and he opened his arms and shrugged. "It's exactly like he says man. Crazy stuff."

Satisfied with Beto's response, Brick continued with the story. "So the meat guy begins shouting to Crazy Cono, 'Hey, I caught this little prick up here trying to steal from you!' That's when Beto came running around the corner with his shoulders down. He hit the big man so hard that he flew into the doorway. Then Ruth came out of nowhere and kicked him right in his face. He groaned like a girl and he felt his mouth to see how many teeth he was missing. Ruth helped me to my feet and we bolted out the door. We've been trying to make it here ever since. The cops are out all over the place trying to find us. But hey, here we are!"

Brick reached into his inside pocket.

"And although the reward is small, we came away with a little something!"

He pulled two beers out and held them up like they were trophies. The group celebrated with boisterous cheers.

"Hold on, hold on," Brick said, quieting everyone. "That's not all." He pulled out the fifty-dollar bill the fat man dropped in the scuffle. "Now we've got plenty of money for next weekend!"

Ruth stepped forward and wrapped her arms around Brick. "I think we should go back in a few days and kick the crap out of the fat son of a bitch just so he knows to mind his own business next time!"

Macho stepped forward and pushed her shoulder. "First off, you need to watch your mouth. All you do is curse and it makes you sound like a jerkoff. And secondly, you need to stop trying to kick everyone's ass. I say we stay away from there until things blow over."

That had been five years ago, and in Ruth's mind, it could've been yesterday or today. It really didn't matter. They were disrespected and that was unforgivable. The belief they made a mistake that day by not settling the score with him had bothered her and finally those feelings were being validated.

As she observed the meat man, she couldn't help but notice how much fatter he looked. He waddled when he walked and she was surprised he didn't drop dead of a heart attack when he ran next to that white car.

She watched him hand something to the woman and she had no doubt that it was the license plate number to the car she drove.

"Good luck with that one, asshole," she said, and started the car. She made a U-turn and felt a surge of regret that she didn't protest Macho's decision not to go after him and teach him a lesson right then and there. But if there was anything she had learned since then, it was that it was never too late to settle old scores.

chapter 2

"THAT FAT FREAKING slob doesn't know when to mind his own business," Ruth stewed and drummed her fingers on the steering wheel. She stared into the heavy flow of traffic, and although she could see the vehicles around her and respond to their actions, her focus was buried deep within, concentrated on what angered her.

"I'm going to get him. I'll make him pay," she said and started to formulate a plan. She wanted a cigarette badly, knowing it would help her think.

"I won't let him get away with disrespecting me again. No way in hell am I going to let that happen."

Ruth lit a cigarette and took a long drag.

"I'm surrounded by a bunch of stupid people that don't listen to reason. Maybe he doesn't know what good advice is even if it were to come up to slap him upside his head."

The approaching traffic light turned yellow and soon changed to red.

"I have to make sure that Brick doesn't find out about this," she said. "If he gets into any trouble, he goes right back to prison and this time he'll go away for a long time. I haven't even gotten him back yet and I'm not willing to risk losing him again over something so stupid. I've been handling things just fine since both of them have been gone and there's no reason why I can't handle this on my own."

As she came upon the red light, Ruth noticed it at the last second and slammed on the brakes. The car skidded into the center of the intersection and settled in a cloud of burnt rubber. The engine knocked, sputtered and stalled.

"Not again," she said and pounded her fist off of the steering wheel.

A tap on her window drew her attention.

"Are you alright?" a gray-haired businessman said. His face was rosy red from the cold and rife with wrinkles. His eyes were gentle and a genuine look of concern covered his face.

Ruth rolled her window down. "Do I look like I need your help?"

He hesitated. "Excuse me, I was just making sure—"

"Ah," she said and waved a dismissive hand at him. "You're a concerned father of someone, I get it. Mine mistreated my mother and left my family when I was a kid. Why don't you do yourself a favor old man and mind your own damn business? I'm having a crappy day and I don't need a sincere old fart like you trying to soften me all up. Got it?"

"If someone had been driving through that intersection you could have killed them."

"Yeah, well, and if my aunt had balls she would have been my uncle."

"I think you should try and be more careful. That's all I'm trying to say."

"Did I ask you for your opinion? Even once?"

"You have a terrible attitude, young lady," he said, pulled his coat closed and walked back to his car.

Ruth hung out the window. "Yeah, I should be good, stand up straight, stay in line, shut my mouth and everything will be fine like a good little donkey!"

The businessman heaved a sigh, shook his head, and got into his car. He drove away, staring at her as he passed by.

"That dumbass doesn't know when to shut his mouth and walk away either," she muttered and started her car.

If she didn't have so much to do, she would have followed him so she could find out where he lived or where he worked. That would give her the opportunity to etch a message into the hood of his car. It would be a simple reminder that he should learn to mind his own business.

RUTH PULLED UP to a trailer with tall grass and a cracked, uneven walkway. A broken-down Ford sat in the oil-stained driveway and had four flat tires.

She tooted the horn and waited several impatient minutes for Alvaro to emerge from the house.

When he didn't appear after a few moments, she laid on the horn again, but this time for several seconds. In an instant, a tall, barrel-shaped guy came to the door in a white tank top and basketball shorts. He held up a finger to signify the brief time it would take him to join Ruth. He disappeared inside the trailer.

Reappearing with a jacket on, he ran from the trailer and jumped inside the car. He cranked up the heat and greeted her with a kiss on the cheek. "Man, it's cold out there."

"As a witch's tit," she said.

He smiled and his metallic teeth gleamed in the orange glow of the setting sun. "What's up?"

"I'm chillin', Alvaro," she said, fetching gum from her purse. "I'm a little shaken up though."

"From what?"

"I nearly got into a crash with your car, man. It was like that close," she said, and held her fingers an inch apart.

Alvaro lifted his rear off the seat and looked down the hood of the car.

Ruth sighed and rolled her eyes. "I said almost, Alvaro. I mean, give me some credit with my driving skills, would you?"

She offered Alvaro a piece of gum and he declined.

"I have to tell you something, but before I do, you have to promise me you're not going to get Brick involved in any way," she said.

Alvaro sighed.

"Or better yet, I need to make sure Macho doesn't find out either. Can you do that for me?" she said.

"You know they don't like it when you do this, Ruth. They told me next time you asked me to do you a favor that I needed to let them know. They warned me, even made me promise."

Ruth sighed and chewed her gum with loud chomps. "Is that what they said?"

He nodded. "They don't want you causing any trouble. They were serious about keeping things quiet for a while now that Brick is out."

"You know what? You can just forget it then, okay? I guess it really doesn't matter what happened to me. Keep your damn promise to them and crap all over me. Shit Alvaro, I mean really!"

Alvaro fell into silence and it was obvious to Ruth that he was weighing her words. She hid a smile, confident that his strong sense of dedication to everyone in the gang would get the better of him.

"Alright, I'm sorry," he said. "I want you to tell me what happened."

"No, thank you. I don't need you running to them and starting all sorts of crap because you've made a ridiculous promise to them."

Alvaro shook his head. "Lighten up on the guilt trip. I get it, okay? I shouldn't have said that and I won't tell Brick or Macho anything about what you're going to tell me. I promise."

She stared at him. "Is this the same type of promise you made to them?"

Alvaro sighed. "Come on, don't give me the opportunity to change my mind about this. Just tell me what happened."

"Promise me and mean it that you won't tell them. This is serious and I know they'll freak out and want to kill this guy. Brick and Macho can't get into any more trouble or they'll go away for good."

Alvaro nodded. "Okay, I promise."

"I'm sorry," she said, looked away and began to cry. "I don't ever let anything get to me. But this . . ."

"You're concerning me now. You need to tell me what's going on."

"This guy—"

"What guy, Ruth? Was it Beto again?"

Ruth shook her head. "No, it wasn't Beto. Why does everyone always assume it's him?"

"Because for a while, it was always him."

"Well, it's not."

"Who then?"

"It was that fat butcher guy next to Cono's deli."

"What happened?" Alvaro said with a puffed chest. "What did he do?"

Ruth sniffed away the tears and took Alvaro by the hands. She looked him in the eyes and blinked hard. "He backed me into a corner and told me he knows who I am and remembers what I did. He grabbed my tit really hard and told me he could do anything he wanted to me and that I couldn't stop him. It was horrible."

She pulled her hands away and covered her eyes and sobbed uncontrollably.

Alvaro turned askew, his eyes bright with rage. "He did what? When did this happen?"

"Just now," she said. "I was in such shock that I almost wrecked. I didn't know where else to go."

"I'm glad you came to me."

"I know I can trust you."

"Yes, you can."

"He licked the side of my face," she said and wiped her cheek. "I can't get the smell of his spit off of me."

"I'll kill him! I'll go there right now and I'll beat his brains in! Do you want to watch while I do that?"

"No, wait," she said and touched him gently. "Let's think this through, okay? I want him to pay, but we need to make sure we don't get sloppy."

Alvaro nodded. "Okay. Tell me what you want me to do then."

chapter 3

JENNIFER PULLED INTO a long sinuous driveway and eased the white BMW into the usual spot next to the well-lit elaborate marble fountain. Turning the engine off, she stepped out of the car, looked at the three-story home and finally felt safe. She opened the back door of the car and unbuckled the harness systems on the booster seats.

"We're home," she said with cheer, trying to make light of the recent events.

She helped Emily and Hannah out of the car.

"Let's get into the house quickly, before the cold gets you."

The dent in the quarter panel was deep and was going to be impossible to hide from Rainer. He would see it and start asking a hundred questions. Before he did, she would need to tell him what happened.

Hurrying the children into the house, Rainer was in the kitchen, snacking on apple slices.

"How are my little girls?" he said, and scooped them up. He twirled them around and the girls talked over each other, both trying to tell their version of the story about the frightening woman they encountered.

"Wait a second, girls," he said and warbled his head and crossed his eyes. "I can't understand what you are saying if you try and speak over each other. One at a time please."

"Girls," Jennifer said before they could tell their father anything. Her hair was windblown and her expression drooped down into a frazzled frown. She pulled off her jacket and set it on the back of a chair. "I would like you both to go upstairs and pick out your pajamas. Mrs. Amanda is coming and I want you to be ready before she arrives."

"But, mom!" the girls protested at the same time.

"I want to talk to dad first," Hannah said.

"Yeah," Emily said. "We want to tell him about the bad woman."

"Not now," Jennifer said. "I would like you both to do as I said."

Rainer set the girls down and gave them a pat on the backsides. "Why don't you go on upstairs and do as your mother asks. I'll be up in a few minutes to help out."

"But dad!"

"Emily, please," he said.

Jennifer watched the girls scurry away and when they were out of sight, she began to straighten an already immaculate countertop.

"Are you okay?" Rainer said, and just watched her. Everything about her seemed frantic and he moved slow and wrapped his arms around her. He gave her a gentle squeeze and it was enough to make her stop fidgeting.

Jennifer resisted him but not too much. "I'm alright," she said. "Tonight is your night and I don't want to take anything away from it."

Her body trembled.

"You're shaking," Rainer said, and tightened his hug. He kissed her neck and nestled his chin into her shoulder. "My night will be ruined if you don't share your troubles with me."

Jennifer sighed and faced Rainer. "Sometimes I don't know where my mind is. I did something really stupid."

He stood up straight. "What is it, honey?"

Jennifer turned away, ashamed of what she was about to tell him. "I was so frustrated with the traffic and I was running late. All I wanted to do is beat you home so I could make sure everything was perfect for you."

"It's perfect."

"No, it's not."

"You're hard on yourself, sweetheart. You shouldn't put so much pressure on yourself."

"I tried to take a shortcut home and I stupidly pulled out into this busy intersection. I didn't look and I almost got into a terrible car accident. I could have gotten the children hurt, and even hurt other people."

Rainer reached out and touched her hands. "You didn't do it on purpose and the important thing is everyone is okay."

Jennifer nodded. "I don't want to upset you, but the car has a pretty big dent."

Rainer made his way to the window to inspect the car. "I'm not following," he said gently. "You said you almost got into a car accident and yet you're telling me the car has a dent?"

Jennifer joined him at the window and pointed. "Driver's side by the front wheel."

Rainer found the dent and dismissed it with a wave of his hand. "I can have that fixed tomorrow, no problem."

"I knew that was what you were going to say," Jennifer said.

Rainer looked at her unevenly.

"Emily was climbing out of her booster seat again," Jennifer said, her back now to Rainer. "She did it when we were at this intersection with a blinking light. I told her she's not allowed out of her seat and she started to argue with me."

"What did she say?"

Jennifer thought in a moment of silence and resigned her search with a shrug. "I don't remember, but I'm sure I was overly sensitive because of the day I was having. I became so furious at her that I actually smacked her." Her eyes welled with tears and she looked at Rainer. "I didn't do it hard, but it was hard enough that it scared us both and I felt terrible about it. I promised myself I would never hit my child."

"I know you did, but it's okay. Sometimes emotions can get the better of us

"I appreciate you saying that, but it's not okay. Afterwards I got her back into her seat and faced forward. I don't know why, but I stomped on the gas pedal and sped right into the intersection. This approaching car skidded around me and—," she shivered, "—this young girl no older than twenty-five got out of her car and started screaming at me. She was shouting obscenities at me, yelling at the children and demanding I get out of the car. She threatened to hurt me. When I refused to get out of the car, she kicked the quarter panel and left that dent."

Rainer moved to comfort his wife. "But you and the kids are safe, and that's what's most important to me. I'm proud of you for not getting out of the car. That would have been dangerous. I'm glad that you kept your cool and were thinking clearly."

Jennifer wiped her tears. "She was so mean and aggressive. I've never seen anything like it. The children were terrified."

"Someone like that doesn't know how gentle you are," Rainer said. "And if she did, I don't know if that would have even made a difference. Some people are just mean."

She nodded. "I know. This really big guy that owns the butcher shop on the corner of that intersection witnessed everything. He gave me the license plate number and I put it in the glove box."

"Well, I think we should reward him somehow for stepping forward. There aren't many people that would be willing to do that nowadays. I think we should call the police so we can get a report filled out."

Rainer reached for the phone.

"No," Jennifer said and placed a hand on top of his hand, stopping him. "Of all nights, tonight is supposed to be a night filled with joy and celebration. If it's all right with you, I'd like to put this behind me and forget about it. At least for the evening."

Rainer nodded and took his hand away from the phone. "If that's what you want, then that is what I want too," he said and kissed her head. He walked towards the stairs. "I have a good feeling about the fundraiser this evening. I'm going to start getting ready. Take as long as you need to gather yourself. Just keep in mind that my brother will be here in less than an hour. If he senses you're upset about something, he's going to pry."

She nodded. "I know he will."

"I love you," he said, and started up the stairs. "And I'm glad no one was hurt."

"Rainer?" Jennifer said, her worried tone made him pause. He looked at her and gave her the time she needed to figure out what she wanted to say.

"Can you do me a favor and don't say anything to your brother about what happened, even if he pries? You know how gung-ho he is about catching the bad guys. I don't want a million questions and having to listen to him insisting on filling out a report and talking to his buddies. I just want to have a good time tonight. That's all I want."

"I cross my heart and hope to die," he said. "You're my wife and I would do anything to protect you."

"Thank you," she said, and her smile slowly returned.

chapter 4

THE DOORBELL RANG and Bach's Symphony No. 5, Allegro con brio filled the household.

"I'll get it," Amanda said, and hurried through the spacious living room and to the door. She looked at the children. "I think your aunt and uncle are here. You guys better hide."

Amanda was a long-time family friend and dependable babysitter and the only one Jennifer trusted with the twins.

In response to Amanda's warning, Emily and Hannah sprang from the couch and shouted as they searched for a secure hiding spot.

Amanda giggled at their frantic scramble and waited until they settled down behind the couch. They giggled, seeming unable to contain themselves.

"What's with all the noise?" Jennifer said, entering the living room with a big smile. She wore an elegant gown and her long red hair bounced with every step.

Amanda moved a finger to her lips. "Shh, they're here. You know—" she winked "—them."

"Oh!" Jennifer said, her eyes wide with understanding. "Hey girls, you are going to need to settle down and keep quiet if you don't want him to hear you."

The girls fell silent with a few random giggles that echoed throughout the lavish house. Jennifer shushed the girls one last time and chased away her smile. She nodded at Amanda.

"Ready or not, here they come," Amanda said, and opened the door.

Dressed in formalwear, Glenn and Stefanie stood arm in arm and a cheerful smile showed their excitement for the evening's event.

Glenn was always proud of his brother's achievements and was never quiet about it either. Anywhere he went, he would tell people that his brother was a surgeon and a celebrated member of the community. But he often told Rainer that he was most proud of the fact that he was a faithful father of two beautiful, well-mannered twin girls and had the perfect marriage to a polite, attractive wife that always turned heads and held people's attention. He openly envied that, and loved being a part of it.

They stepped inside the house and Glenn moved stiffly in the tuxedo. He pulled at his lapel, but held onto his smile.

"My oh my, don't you look handsome!" Jennifer said to Glenn, and stepped forward with a warm hug and kiss.

"Ah," Glenn smiled and waved a dismissive hand at his sister-in-law. "You just like to say that to try and distract me. But I know it's because you don't want that other side of me to come out."

She laughed. "Now what could you be talking about?"

"You know what I'm talking about! There are children in here and I'll bet you they're hiding."

"Children?" Jennifer said, and batted her eyes and looked around the room. "I don't see any children around."

"I can feel a change coming on and I can't resist it."

"A change you say? What sort of change could you be talking about?"

He howled like a wolf. "Kids are near! I can smell them and it makes my stomach growl!"

Jennifer and Stefanie laughed as Glenn hunched into a feral position.

"I wouldn't lie to you Mr. Wolf," Jennifer said. "There aren't any children here. Isn't that so?" she said to Amanda.

Amanda nodded and held back a laugh. "That's right, there are no kids here," she said, and scurried into the kitchen.

Glenn sniffed the air. "You can't hide them from me. I know they're here somewhere. They're in a place where they think they're safe, but they are not!"

He growled and started down the hallway and exaggerated his search for the girls with long, heavy footsteps and deep breaths and heavy exhales.

The twins screamed as they emerged from their hiding spots and danced around their uncle. They latched onto his legs and he dragged them down the hallway, pretending they weren't even there.

JENNIFER AND STEFANIE sat on the couch and watched Glenn drag the kids into the playroom. Stefanie turned her attention away from Glenn and the children. Her smile quickly faded and she sighed, long and deliberate.

"Are you okay?" Jennifer said, and had suspected that their conversation would move in this direction but not quite so soon. Rainer had forewarned this might happen after a recent conversation he had with his brother. Of course Rainer asked his wife to pretend she didn't know anything, and that was what she was going to do.

"It's really nice to see Glenn so animated," Stefanie said, her voice was low and her eyes were sad. "Whenever we're coming to see you guys, he just glows with excitement. He has so much love and admiration for you, Rainer and the children."

"Is it still happening?"

Stefanie nodded. "It seems more frequently now."

Jennifer placed a hand on Stefanie's knee. "I'm so sorry you have to go through this. I know how difficult this must be for the both of you."

"It is," Stefanie said, and she sighed. "I wish I could explain what this has done to the love we have for each other and what it is doing to our marriage. We hardly have a meaningful conversation anymore let alone any sexual contact. You can't imagine how hurtful it is to hear your husband tell you that he doesn't see a reason for it. I feel so unattractive."

"Oh Stefanie, I'm so sorry. You're such a beautiful woman."

"It's as if it has destroyed all of our emotional connections. If it's not dead quiet around the house, it's a finger-pointing screaming match about who is to blame for this."

Jennifer watched Stefanie and she could see how deep her sorrow was. She seemed tired and had attempted to cover dark rings that hung beneath her eyes with a thick layer of makeup. There were plenty of gray hairs mixed within the shoulder-length brown that hadn't existed six months ago.

"I'm sorry," Stefanie said, and stood. "I shouldn't be putting this on you. This is supposed to be a night of celebration. Not this silly drama."

"I'm here for you. We're family, and if we can't count on each other, then we can't count on anyone," Jennifer said.

Although Jennifer meant what she said, an awkward silence filled the room and she felt like she needed to say something, anything that might help them through the moment, but stopped herself.

"What?" Stefanie said.

"Nothing. Forget it."

"No, you were going to say something and I need to hear what it was."

Jennifer licked her lips. "I don't know if the time is ever going to be right for me to say this, but Rainer has this doctor friend that's a fertility specialist—"

"No," Stefanie said. The abruptness of her tone made Jennifer feel as though she crossed some invisible line of right and into wrong.

"I'm sorry, I didn't mean that to sound so harsh," Stefanie said. "That is something that's not going to work. I've suggested we see a fertility doctor and even suggested we look into adoption." She bit her lip. "Glenn was infuriated when I suggested it. That's why I don't dare go there again. That caused one of the worst arguments we had. No matter what I do, I can't get him to understand or even accept that if we don't go to a specialist, we will never know what the source of the problem is. But more importantly I've learned that if I keep my mouth shut, it tends to keep the peace."

The sound of small running feet and shrieks of laughter rumbled through the hallway towards Stefanie and Jennifer. The children broke into the room and scrambled for a place to hide. Glenn emerged from the hallway and a low growl accompanied his slow pace. The women separated and Jennifer spotted Rainer coming down the stairs.

"Hurry," Jennifer said, and pointed at Rainer. "Run to your father, he'll save you!"

Rainer reached his arms out and descended the stairs two at a time. The twins ran to him. "I've got you," he said, and scooped them up. "I'll protect you from that monster!"

"Rainer, I think we should get going," Jennifer said. She tapped her finger against her wristwatch. "We're cutting it close." She stood and grabbed her jacket. "Showing up late to an event you organized wouldn't make the best impression."

Rainer smirked. "We have plenty of time. Besides, if we're running late, we can always get a police escort." He turned to his brother, winked at him and bumped shoulders with him. "Isn't that right?"

"That's right," Glenn said and puffed his chest.

"Please don't encourage him," Stefanie said and nudged Rainer with an elbow.

"Mommy?" Emily said. "Uncle Glenn told me he caught a bad guy today and brought him to jail."

"Is that so?" Jennifer said and looked at Glenn.

"That's right," Glenn said and placed his hands on his hips.

"That's because he's big and strong like daddy," Hannah said, and she made a muscle.

"Wow, look at the size of that thing!" Stefanie said, and gave Hannah's bicep a gentle squeeze.

Rainer looked at his younger brother and then back at Hannah. "You have big muscles just like your uncle. That's why none of the bad guys can get away from him. Maybe you can be a policeman when you get older. Would you like that?"

"I can't be a policeman, dad. I would be a policewoman."

"Of course," Rainer said and everyone laughed. He hugged his daughters and put them down. "We have to get going now. I want you to be good for Amanda and listen to her. Remember, she's in charge."

"We know that, daddy," Emily said. "You say that every time."

"Your father and I love you both very much," Jennifer said and hugged the children. She went over the list of contacts with Amanda one last time.

Glenn crouched into the feral position again, and spoke with his monster voice. "Don't forget that I love you too!" he growled, and the children screamed and ran away.

RUTH STEERED HER car onto a dirt driveway and sounded the horn twice. She stalled the engine and hopped out of the car. Hurrying across trampled weeds and patches of dirt, she shouted, "Brick!"

Brick emerged from a singlewide trailer wearing a stained white tank top and torn, dirty blue jeans. He ran towards Ruth. "Oh my god, Ruth!"

The two met in the center of the lawn and Brick swept her up and spun her around.

"I can't believe you're here," he said.

"Squeeze tighter then," she said and kissed the side of his unshaven face and wrapped her arms around his neck. "I came as soon as I heard you'd gotten out. You should've called me. I could've picked you up and made a good meal for you."

Brick put her down and pounded his plump belly proudly. "I ain't starving, and besides, I didn't want to put you out."

Ruth slapped his shoulder. "You didn't want to put me out? What the hell did they do to you in there, turn you into a damn sissy?"

"Did they turn you into a sissy," he mocked in a high-pitched voice. "Oh, they took your balls too?"

"Yeah, and they fed them to your mother."

They laughed.

"Let's go inside and crack a few cold ones," he said.

Ruth released the anger she had been harboring since she heard about his release. It no longer mattered that he didn't call her right away. Within his deep blue eyes she saw the intensity and resilience of ten men. And in his arms she felt the strength and comfort of twenty. It was a feeling she had missed and often longed for.

"I could so use a drink, you have no idea," she said, and smiled at the inevitability of the coming buzz.

"Being locked away for as long as I have? Yeah, I have an idea," Brick said, and put his arm around her and pulled her close.

The strength.

"Wanna go to Soren's tonight?" he said and raised a brow.

"Does a bear shit in the woods?"

They laughed.

"He called me less than an hour after I got home and said he was having a party. He said it is in celebration of my release."

Ruth wrapped her arm around his waist and clung to the comfort of his nearness. "Well, I like your idea of having a few now. I guess we can look at it as getting a head start."

"I only have a six-pack in the fridge. We can stop off on the way to the party and get some more for the ride in. The last one inside buys the beers!"

He ran for the door, swung it open and jumped inside the trailer. Thrown clothes, empty cans, bottles, and displaced items cluttered the inside of the small trailer. "I hope you've been saving your pennies, because you're buying."

Ruth climbed the steps with an unhappy look on her face. "I see you're still a jackass!" she said.

"Maybe, but I'm a jackass that doesn't have to pay. Now go and sit your ass down and I'll get us something to drink." He pushed a pile of clothes off the bed and onto the floor.

Ruth threw herself onto the bed and her feet dangled on the floor. Brick reentered the room with two beers and cracked them open. He handed Ruth hers and quickly chugged his. A roaring belch filled the room and Ruth laughed heartily. Brick plopped himself on the bed next to her.

"I don't know why you're bothering to sit. I'm ready for the next round," she said, and chugged her beer as quickly as he did.

Brick watched her and a growing smile took over his face. "What are you, a knockdown drunk or something? You should be ashamed of yourself," he said, and he left the room with a laugh.

"Just like your daddy," Ruth said, and burped loud and long. "I learned from the best."

Brick entered the room with a wide smile that lit up his face. "And you're a damn pig besides. Belching like you're a damn man."

"Hey, suck mine. It's okay when you do it, but I can't because I'm a girl?" She took the beer from Brick and fell to her back. She coolly slipped a hand behind her head and rested the beer on her stomach. She stared at the ceiling in contemplation and chuckled.

"What?" Brick said. His smile disappeared, and a look of curiosity turned him serious.

Ruth liked what she saw and sat up and slowed things down with a long pause before she spoke. "I was just thinking how much I've missed you and your antics."

Brick allowed the smile to return. "Yeah, well, and I've missed you and yours."

"I was thinking about the time me, you, and Beto went on the beer run and the fat meat man came after us."

"Yeah," Brick laughed. "That was something great. But it seems like it was a lifetime ago and he is someone I would prefer we both forget."

He fell silent.

"Are you okay?" she said.

"Yeah man, I'm fine. Those prison cells give you plenty of time to think."

"About what?"

"I don't know. Like the things in the past that were left undone. But the past is the past and I want to leave it there."

"You hold onto shit way too long."

"Are you defending him? Is that what you're getting at?"

"No. Don't be stupid. I'm just saying what I'm thinking."

"Have you seen him since I went in?"

"No," she said. "I wouldn't do that to you or myself."

Brick nodded while he sipped his beer. "And that's the truth?"

"Yeah, that's the truth. Don't be such a damn buzz kill."

"Okay, that's cool then."

"So why didn't you call me as soon as you got out?" she said. "I was getting really pissed at you. I was waiting to see how long it would take before you decided to give me a call."

Brick sat on a torn garbage bag filled with clothes. As he sunk, the bag released a musty smell. He leaned into the wall and raised an eyebrow. "Actually, I was going to surprise you by being at the party tonight. Alvaro was supposed to get you to come."

Ruth's face lit up. "Oh, that's really cute." She planted a kiss on his cheek. "Speaking of Alvaro, he told me to tell you that he was gonna be a little late tonight. Something suddenly came up that needed his attention."

Brick stared at her. "So, you knew about the party already?"

Ruth laughed and jumped off of the bed and straddled Brick's legs; she had him right where she wanted him. She made a fist and playfully thrust her knuckles at his chin. She pushed him and sent him toppling over.

"So what if I did?" she said. "Do you have a problem with that?"

Brick settled on his back and held his beer high. "Just for the record, I didn't spill a single drop."

Ruth laughed and moved to the door.

"Out-of-shape drunks usually don't," Ruth said, and bowed. "One point for me."

Brick jumped up. "I am no drunk and I'm in good shape," he laughed and pushed out his gut. "Last I heard round was a shape." He finished his second beer. "And I believe that is two for me and only one for you."

He crushed and then discarded the empty can.

chapter 5

RAINER ADJUSTED THE rearview mirror and checked the proximity of his brother's car. The candy apple red SUV that Glenn drove followed close behind and he turned his eyes back to the road.

"Did you get a chance to speak to Stefanie about Doctor Grimbar?" Rainer said to Jennifer.

She nodded. "I tried, but she crushed the idea before I could complete the sentence. She said that every time she tries to speak to Glenn about the subject, things get really heated and really ugly."

Rainer returned his attention to the rearview mirror and studied his brother's car as if the answer to his confusion was written in the gleam of the headlights.

"He's always been a bit pigheaded," Rainer said. "If what Stefanie is saying is the truth, I would have to say he's being irrational. I don't get why he's so resistant to the idea."

Jennifer shrugged. "I don't know. If he's sterile, maybe he feels as though he's less of a man or an unfit mate."

Rainer looked at Jennifer and raised an eyebrow. The displeasure of having to hear his wife say that about his brother irritated him. "Why would you draw such conclusions? If he is sterile, that doesn't make him any less of a man or an unfit mate."

"I know that. I'm not attacking him in any way," she said.

Although his wife always kept a calm and even tone when she spoke to him, at times, her logic was hard to listen to. "That's not how it sounds to me."

"I'm sorry," Jennifer said gently. "That might have come across as a bit crass."

Rainer nodded. "Thank you for saying that."

Jennifer smiled and rubbed his thigh. "I know how much you love your brother and that you want him to be happy. It's just that someone in a position like his might have the potential to feel like their life was a bit . . . complicated? I don't know, I'm certain a lot of self-doubt plays a big part on the outbursts of anger he's been having."

"You should have kept your practice," Rainer said, his irritation gone. "You're a great therapist and there are a lot of people that would benefit from your help."

She shook her head. "I wanted to start a family. I don't regret that decision."

Rainer smiled. "Neither do I. That was one of your best ideas."

"Yes it was," she said, and shook her head agreeably.

"I'm curious to know if Stefanie said something to you that made you come to that conclusion?" he said.

"I'm not sure what you're asking me."

"Did she say that Glenn told her he felt like he was less of a man or that he's a terrible mate to her?"

"No," she said, and shook her head. "But I know that's a strong possibility of why he might be acting out."

"Even though I know you don't mean to, your words sound so harsh and terrible."

"I know it does. But maybe this will help you look at what they're going through from a different angle. Your brother has a lot of confused emotions stirring around inside that he's afraid to face. I don't know, he might believe if he was to discover the answer, then his worst fears might become realized. Ultimately, I think that is what he's trying to avoid."

Rainer sat in a rising swell of frustration that was accompanied by sympathy and helplessness for his brother. "Yeah, but so what, what if he's sterile?"

"Rainer?" she said.

"That doesn't make him any less of a man than anyone I know!"

"I know that. We know that. But this is something he still has to figure out."

He shook his head. "That is not what fatherhood is about. The real job comes when you have to care for them and instill values and principles that will help carry them throughout their entire adult lives."

"Everything you're saying is true, but you're able see that because you're not in the same predicament as him."

"But I am in it with him. I only wish there was something I could do to help him."

She looked at Rainer with the same sympathy he had for his brother. "I want you to know that you're right in your point of view and I even believe what you're saying, but we're wrong in his. You are a parent of two beautiful children. You get to experience joys he may never have the opportunity to. When your daughters smile at you, you can see a part of you in their smile."

"This isn't making me feel any better about it."

"No, but if you gain some understanding, you might figure out a way to help him. You two are so close, he may open up to you. You've always had a special connection."

He nodded his acceptance. "I know."

"Now, could you imagine, I mean really imagine them having the twins and we were unable to have children of our own?" She paused and sighed. "To even try and imagine it bothers me so much that I could cry. But what I want you to think about is if we were unable to have children and we really wanted them, and you found out you were sterile, how do you think it would make you feel? I want you to dig deep before you answer me."

She turned to stare out the passenger window. "It's an unpleasant thought, I know. But if I'm going to be honest, I know I would be outright confused, angry and probably even a little ashamed."

Rainer sighed and loosened the tightening grip he had on the steering wheel. He submitted his frustration to understanding. "I guess I can see what you're getting at."

"No," Jennifer said softly. "I think you can finally see where his anger is coming from."

EDDIE GATHERED THE trimmings of meat and fat and placed them in a bucket that would be used to make chop meat. He wiped the countertop clean of blood and whistled while he worked. A persistent knock on the door drew his attention but he carried on with his closing procedures, acting as though he didn't hear the sound. He rinsed the rag and watched the blood swirl around the sink and disappear down the drain.

The knock at the door came again, but this time it was much louder and more persistent.

"I'm closed," he shouted over his shoulder and shook his head. "Damn people always wait until the last minute. I've had the same business hours for years."

Another barrage of knocks at the door forced his attention and he tossed the bloodstained rag onto the counter and it landed with a wet plop. Outside the door, a little old lady bundled up tight against the cold sweeping wind waved at him.

Eddie felt the embarrassment of having spoken to an elderly person in such a tone redden his cheeks. He hurried to the door and unlocked it. He poked his head outside and said, "I'm sorry, miss, but I'm closing up for the night."

"Oh," the frail woman said. She pointed at her car across the parking lot and moved her finger to the sign hanging in the window. "I only got out of my car and walked all the way over here because the sign in your window says you're still open."

Eddie looked at the sign, and to his dismay, it did say he was open for business.

"I'm really sorry about that," he said, unable to turn her away. "Please, come on inside. What can I get for you?"

"I don't want to keep you. I'll come back tomorrow," she said, and started to retreat.

"Please, it's the least I can do after you made the trip out here and I left you standing out in the cold. It will be my pleasure to get you what you need."

She paused and turned to face him, moving stiffly. "You'd do that for me?"

He was reminded of his own mother and it tugged on his heartstrings. "It's the least I can do," he said with a smile.

"Okay. If you insist, but I want you to know I would have come back tomorrow. I know exactly what I want and it shouldn't take more than a minute or two."

"That's not a problem," he said, and held the door open for her. She moved and watched every step as she entered the shop. Moving with a slow waddle, she settled in front of the display case and scanned the glass for her selection. She tugged on her chin while she did so. "It is very nice of you to let me in. I mean it, you didn't have to do that."

"Yes, I did," he said, and locked the door. He turned the sign around and double-checked that it said he was closed. Walking behind the counter, he said, "Have you made a decision?"

"I'm looking for a roast that's about three pounds with a little bit of fat left on it."

Eddie searched the meat case and found the roast he felt was the best match to what she described. He held it up for her to see. "How is this one?"

She stared at the roast in a long moment of contemplation. "No, I don't think that will do. I have company coming and I think I would like it to have a little more fat on it. It helps with the flavor. And also, maybe you can find one that is a little more squared. That helps me cook it evenly while retaining the tenderness of the meat."

Eddie hid his face behind the frame of the display case and rolled his eyes. Letting her inside might have been the biggest mistake he's made all day.

"ARE YOU SURE the door was locked?"

"Yeah," Alvaro said, breathing heavy. "It was locked."

"But the sign says he's still open."

"C'mon man, think," Alvaro said to Chico. He now sat next to him in the car. "He obviously forgot to turn the sign around when he locked up for the night."

Chico nodded and they watched an old lady park her car, walk to the butcher shop and try the door.

"Maybe she'll get him to realize that and create an opportunity for me," Alvaro said. "Either way, he's got to come outside eventually."

The old woman knocked on the glass door.

"She's persistent, I'll give her that," Chico said.

"That's good for us," Alvaro said. "I want you to follow her home. We're going to need to have a talk with her after this is all over with. We have to make sure that she didn't see us and there are no loose ends."

"I can do that," he said and cracked his knuckles. "Do you think I should put the fear of God into her? I don't know, maybe punch her around a little bit?"

Alvaro shook his head. "I don't even want her to know that she's being followed. The only thing I want you to do is find out where she lives. This is a just-in-case scenario."

Chico's shoulders went limp and he sighed.

"Relax," Alvaro said and slapped his friend's shoulder. "You'll get your chance at some action soon enough."

"I hope so," Chico said, sitting up straight. "I've been dying to get in on the . . ."

The meat man poked his head outside and engaged in a conversation with the old woman, stealing their attention.

"Here we go," Alvaro said.

At first it appeared as though he was going to turn her away, but then he opened the door and let her inside. The meat man peered out the window and they slid down in their seats. Flipping the window sign to "closed," the meat man turned away.

"That's him?" Chico said.

"Yeah man, that's him. I want you to remember to keep your mouth shut about this. No one can know we were here—not even Brick."

"I know."

"No one!"

Chico raised a brow to Alvaro. "Do you think I'm that dumb that I would go and run my mouth about this? I know this wasn't approved and I know what would happen if they found out what we were doing."

Alvaro smirked and reached for the bat that was in the back seat. "I'm just makin' sure you remembered what you agreed to do here."

"Hey, what exactly did he do to her anyways?"

Alvaro looked at Chico and held the bat out. "Enough to earn him a few swings from this."

"It must have been bad."

Chico was missing an ear, and although Alvaro knew he was self conscious about it, he couldn't help but stare at the torn flesh that was mangled and scarred. It was bit off in a fight. "I'm going to make his face look like that."

"Real funny, man," Chico said, and looked away.

"I ain't joking. He grabbed her and stuff. He didn't treat her like a lady, you know?"

Chico raised a brow and cracked a smile. "I know she's a little chunky, but there's something about her that's real nice."

Alvaro slapped Chico on the back of his head. "I think there's something wrong with you. If Brick heard you saying that, he'd kick the crap out of you. And you wouldn't be able to talk for a month."

"But he's not here and what's happening here right now isn't really happening, right?"

"Yeah man, that's right."

"So what's the problem? Besides, it's not like her to just sit there and take it. What did she do about it?"

"Did you see the size of that guy?"

"Yeah, I did."

"Then what do you think she could do? She came to me and told me what happened. That's why we're here. That's what she did about it."

"I don't know, I've seen her tripping out before. She's crazy, and no matter his size, I'm still surprised she didn't kick him in the balls or something."

"Well, she was crying when she came to me. That's all I know and all I needed. When have you ever seen her cry?"

"Never."

"Yeah, exactly."

"Look," Chico said, and nodded in the direction of the store. "You better get going."

Alvaro watched the meat man escort the old woman to the door. "Don't start your car until she's in hers," he said. "And remember to keep out of sight."

He got out of the car with a firm hold on his bat. Bouncing the lumber off of the palm of his hand a few times, it made a heavy thudding sound. "Stick to the plan. I've got business to take care of."

Alvaro ran across the parking lot and pulled himself against the wall of the adjoining deli shop.

He eyed the old woman and the way she walked all hunched over. It reminded him of his own grandmother and suddenly he wasn't so keen on having to do the things he might have to do to her to keep this clean. But he would do it if he had to.

CHICO WATCHED ALVARO enter the store. He looked at the old woman and watched her struggle with her stiffness as she got into her car.

"Here we go," he said, and started his car. The pounding of his heart quickened and his palms began to sweat.

The old woman slowly pulled out of her parking spot and started down the street.

Chico followed her from a safe distance and glanced at the storefront where he last saw Alvaro. He could see he had already made it inside the store and he was standing behind the meat man. He held the bat by his side, and for a moment, he wished he could switch places with Alvaro. But he convinced himself that what he was doing had importance too.

AN ORNATE DISPLAY of lit candles atop a bouquet of flowers with a ribbon inscribed with the word *hope* decorated the center of every table inside the lavish lyceum. Streamers entwined with Christmas lights hung from the ceiling, giving the illusion of a star-filled night.

The large room was divided into two sides, separated by an aisle and there were twenty-five tables with eight chairs on either side. People from all professions came to fill the seats: doctors, lawyers, investors, corporate CEOs and entrepreneurs. Although they all gathered for gain, this event wasn't for personal gain. It was a show of force for good. It followed the vision of one man and his hope for the betterment of those he came in contact with.

Rainer stepped to a podium at the head of the room and breathed into the microphone to test its volume. He cleared his throat, and said, "I would like to take this opportunity to thank everyone for coming. Your generosity has been a blessing to everyone it has touched and will continue to touch for many months to come."

The people applauded, and Rainer joined them, a proud smile showed his appreciation for what they did, and his enthusiasm for what was to come.

"As most of you know," Rainer continued and the applause quickly quieted. "I've been a surgeon for nearly twelve years now. I replace the marrow in bones for children with the most horrible disease. I am also the lead surgeon on the gunshot trauma team; my focus remains firmly on our policemen and women wounded in the line of duty. That service began when my brother, Glenn, was shot in a botched robbery where a bullet made its way around his vest. He nearly died on the table, and that is when I realized I could assemble a team skilled enough to help save the lives of many men and women that were unfortunate enough to have crossed paths with a monster hell-bent on killing someone over a uniform."

The captain of police stood and applauded. "Thank you, Doctor," he shouted, and soon, everyone was standing and applauding.

"These men and women selflessly place themselves in harm's way to protect us," Rainer shouted over the applause. He raised his hands and moved his mouth close to the microphone. "I'm sorry to keep things so short, but I have something I've been aching to get to."

Everyone sat and Rainer took a sip of water. "As most of you know, I am a proud member of West Maple Hospital. Within the facility, my team members and I run tests and diagnose and treat deathly ill patients. Like the members of my staff, I am on call twenty-four hours a day, seven days a week. We've all made that commitment to ensure anyone in need will get the urgent care they deserve.

"I would like to take a moment to thank my staff, the police that protect us day and night, and the members of the community who continue to work hard and dig deep into their wallets to donate money. I know how much all of you here have given and sacrificed, and for that, you deserve many thanks for it. And to my wife, Jennifer, thank you for not only supporting me and my work, but for being my best friend and a great mother to our beautiful girls."

The people began to applaud again, and Rainer took the moment to throw his wife a kiss. The smile that pulled his lips up showed how much he cared for her.

"With all of the blessings I've had in my life, there isn't much that touches my heart deeper than what I have to share with you, my closest friends, here tonight."

Rainer searched the shelf underneath the podium and came up with a large picture of a bald child lying in bed with machines surrounding him and tubes filling every orifice. Purple rings encircled his sunken eyes, and his pale skin was a sickly shade of yellow. The pain in his eyes was easy to see and they begged for help.

"Everyone, this is Lucas. Lucas had no more than a year to live when he first came to West Maple. When I sat down to talk to him, he told me what he would like to do when he got older. He told me he would like to be a counselor. I think the exact words he said were that he would like to be a counselor to the counselors. He said he would like to help them because he knew how hard it must be for them to watch someone slowly die and not be able to do anything about it. He said he could help them cope with that loss on a daily basis because he was so close to it."

Rainer paused.

"Imagine hearing that. I remember leaving the room after that conversation like it was yesterday. I thought how awful a place this world would be without that boy named Lucas. He was young and genuine in his innocence. He had a deep insight and a profound understanding of the precious gift called life.

"And with your generous donations, in both the past and present, Lucas and others like him can be the counselor or teacher they've always dreamed of becoming. But this day, Lucas wanted to come here to thank you all personally."

Rainer pointed to a door in the rear of the room.

"I'm proud to introduce to you the very brave and courageous ten-year-old boy I consider both a friend and inspiration to us all. Ladies and gentleman, it is my honor to introduce to you, Lucas!"

The door swung open and Lucas came into the lyceum with the aid of crutches. He slowly made his way into the room. Everyone's eyes filled with tears, and they all stood and began to applaud. The volume of the applause grew louder the further into the room he went.

EDDIE TWISTED THE lever and moved the deadbolt back. He flashed his best customer service smile and glanced at his wristwatch. She had taken up nearly twenty minutes of his time.

"Thank you for letting me inside and for being so patient," the old woman said.

"Thank you for your business. Have a wonderful night."

"I will now that I have the perfect roast," the old woman said, and strolled out into the night.

Eddie sighed in relief. He pulled the door closed and turned his attention to the store. The counter was going to need to be wiped down before he could go home. Exhausted and wanting to kick his feet up, watch the game and put this day behind him, he decided that the remainder of his cleaning could wait until he returned in the morning.

The door was pulled open and it tapped closed.

"Damn," Eddie mumbled, realizing he didn't lock the door after he let the old lady out.

"I'm sorry—" he said and faced the customer "—but I'm closed for the evening."

"I'm not here to buy anything from you," a young man that was as big as him said.

"I'm sorry?" Eddie said, and took notice of the bat he raised and rested on his shoulder.

"No, you're not," the young man said and flashed a smile. His silver teeth gleamed in the florescent light. "But you will be."

He swung the bat at Eddie's head.

Clunk!

Eddie saw a flash of light and an intense throbbing pain filled his head. He staggered around a bit, not certain what just happened or what he needed to do. He hadn't been this stunned since the seventh grade when big Tommy Plains sucker punched him. It was strange, this thought, as was his vision that blurred and refocused and then dimmed. A high-pitched buzzing sound filled his ears and he remembered he had to finish cleaning the counter before he could go home.

"You had this coming to you," the voice sounded as though it was underwater. "You should learn to keep your hands to yourself. Now it's time for you to say goodnight."

Eddie was struck a second time. All the pain left his body in an instant, but he couldn't feel his body and everything moved around him precariously, bending and shifting with blots of black and explosive flashes of light. His eyes rolled into the back of his head and he fell forward.

BRICK SEARCHED THE street for a parking spot nearest the party house. After he drove the entire length of the block for the second time, Ruth sighed her frustration.

"I should've driven," she said. She was slouched in her seat and was pulling the label off of her sixth beer since they left his house. "If he isn't courteous enough to reserve a spot out front for us, then we should park on his damn lawn."

"It's not that big of a deal," Brick said.

"Yes, it is," Ruth said. "Why don't you go in the house, find Soren, and give him the keys. Make him find you a parking spot."

"We have the entire night to party. Don't ruin it because of a stupid parking spot."

He held his empty bottle out for her to take.

Ruth eyed it. "You're two behind me."

"I stopped keeping count. Besides, I had to make sure I got you here in one piece."

"We're here, now let's park this thing and get to partying."

She took Brick's empty bottle and returned it to the case carton. "I wonder how I can ruin something that is already starting out crappy. It's freezing out and I don't like having to walk across creation because Soren is a lousy host."

"Why don't I drop you off and I'll go and park the car on my own?"

"That's not what I was suggesting," Ruth said. "I want to stay with you as much as I can."

"It's not a big deal, man. I'll be there in a minute," he said. "Go ahead, I'll meet you."

Brick eased the car to a stop in front of the party house. A continuous flow of people were arriving.

The muddled sound of loud conversation and distorted music could be heard from inside the car. Ruth livened up and sent a smile towards Brick. "But thank you for being so considerate. This is going to be awesome!"

"You know it will," he said, and turned away. "Now get your ass out of the car and have my beer ready when I get inside. I'll be there in a minute."

Ruth kicked the door open and wrappers and cans spilled out onto the street. "I think I should clean the car out before I give it back to Alvaro."

"Yeah, that would be nice."

She turned to Brick with a wry smile. "Imagine something like that happening . . . Not! Don't keep me waiting too long," she said, and slammed the door and hurried across the lawn.

BRICK RAN FROM his car to the house, slowing as he neared the front door. A surge of adrenaline quickened the thump of his heart and he pulled the door open.

Loud music and smoke filled the air. Beer made the floors slick and the acrid aroma of vomit assaulted his senses and even relaxed him some. A sea of people that stood in packed circles carried on with their conversation and he pushed his way into the house. He stood in the middle of the room, raised his arms, and screamed, "Whooh!"

Everyone shouted back and applauded.

"Where's the beer?" Brick said, and people pointed. He moved in that direction.

"What's up, Brick?" someone said and slapped his back.

"It's good to have you back," someone else said.

"Stop by when you get a chance," a faceless someone said, and Brick laughed at the attention he was getting.

"You all make me proud," Brick said without breaking stride. As he advanced, he was flooded with welcoming smiles, continued handshakes, and countless pats on the back.

"Where's the beer?" he said.

"Keep going straight. The kegs are back there."

"Thanks," he said, and continued to push his way through the crowd. By chance he spotted Ruth standing off to the side, leaning against the wall. Her arms were folded across her chest and a guy that wore a black leather trench coat stood close to her. His hair was long and stringy and he was tall and thin. He pointed a finger in her face and she looked away with displeasure.

"Hey!" Brick shouted and felt a desperate sense of urgency to intervene. He pushed people aside until he reached the guy in the leather jacket. He grabbed him by the arm and spun him around. "What do you think you're doing?"

"Hey, Brick, it's good to see you again buddy."

It was Beto and his hair had grown a lot since he last saw him. He had grown a beard that made him look much older than he was.

"You!" Brick said, and he broadened his shoulders. He stepped forward. "I asked you what the hell you were doing!"

Beto looked at Ruth and then back at Brick. "I'm having a word with Ruth."

"I think your conversation with her is over, bitch."

"No, it's not," Beto said, devoid of emotion. "I told you the last time we went through this that I'll speak to whoever I want."

Brick's face was bright red.

"I'm glad you're out and I was hoping we could talk," Beto said. "I want us to put the past behind us, and I'd like to be friends again."

"There's not a chance in hell that's going to happen," Brick said, and shoved Beto. "Now leave. You're not welcome here."

"Relax, man. I'm not against you and I just want to chill and have a couple of beers."

"I remember me and Macho telling you to stay away from her. She doesn't want anything to do with you."

"What happened in the past between me and Ruth was blown way out of proportion."

"You've tried to tell me that before and I'm really not interested in hearing it again. You no longer run with us or have anything to do with her. You'll be smart to remember that."

"What I remember is us making a pact a long time ago," Beto said. "Regardless of what happened between us, I intend to keep my word." Beto turned to Ruth. "I guess now wouldn't be a good time to tell him?"

Ruth shoved Beto. "Don't you try and start any shit tonight, Beto!"

"That's cool," Beto said and took a moment to straighten his jacket. "I'll talk to you soon," he said, and leaned in to kiss her.

Brick lunged forward and grabbed Beto by his throat. He screamed into his face and threw him to the floor. He jumped on top of him and tightened his hold on Beto's neck, punching him in the face and drawing blood.

"I'm telling you right now, if you come around her again," Brick said through clenched teeth, "I swear to God that I will kill you! Now when you find yourself like this again with a knife sticking out of your side, don't say you weren't warned."

Ruth wedged herself between Beto and Brick. "Don't get into it like this, Brick. You just got out and I don't want you going back in because of him. He isn't worth it."

Brick loosened his hold and stood. "So what is it? What didn't you tell me?" Brick said, his eyes focused on Ruth, ablaze with rage. "Were you screwing him again while I was away? Did this start up again?"

Ruth watched some of the partygoers help Beto to his feet. She turned to Brick with fury. "Is that what you think? Don't you know by now he says things like that to screw with your mind?"

Brick stepped towards Beto and kicked him. "I should just kick his dirt bag ass and get it over with."

Ruth fought back against Brick's advancement. "I said not here and certainly not now! Let's move to a different part of the house and try to have a good time."

Brick remained firmly in place. "Maybe you were right. Maybe this night is ruined."

"Why, whenever we go out, does crap like this always have to happen?" she said. "I can't believe you've spent all of that time in jail stewing about him."

BRICK STOOD BY the beer keg and was in conversation with a short round man named Paco.

"Two months before I got out of jail, I watched this guy get his head beat in. He was a snitch and he got what was coming to him," Brick said and worked the tap.

"Was it scary being in there?"

Brick shrugged. "It wasn't that bad. I learned to stick with my own kind and was forced to act a lot of crazy because I learned it was the only way to survive."

Paco refilled his beer. "I got busted having some weed on me not too long ago. The cops pushed me on the hood of my car and were real rough with me. They threatened to take me to jail but took the evidence and told me they were going to cut me a break."

Brick laughed. "I think it was more like they were helping themselves to the goods." He acted like he was taking a hit off a joint. "I hate the police. They're a bunch of crooked bastards! Sometimes I swear I wouldn't hesitate to kill one if I had the chance."

"Me too," Paco said.

"Man, it feels like it has been forever since I've been high. I don't even remember what it is like."

"Well, why don't we go for a ride and see if we can score us some weed. We'll get the good shit. What do you think, do you want to go?"

Brick glanced over Paco's shoulder to see if he could spot Ruth in the crowd. The thick cloud of smoke in the air, the number of people and his own impairment made it impossible for him to locate her.

"Sure I'll go for a ride," he said. "I could use the time away."

"His eye is swollen shut from that punch."

"He deserves a lot worse."

"You let him off easy."

"Don't let me smoke anything because my parole officer warned me about random drug testing."

BRICK OCCUPIED THE passenger seat in Paco's Chevy Blazer. He turned the radio down and gently eased his head on the headrest. Although the vehicle was idle at a red light, he still felt like he was moving.

"Man, I am wrecked," Brick said and the dizzying feeling made him nauseous. "I guess that's what happens when you can't work on your tolerance while you're locked inside of a cage."

"It sounds like you have some work to do," Paco said.

"The way I'm feeling right now, I know I have a lot of work to do."

"You've been pounding them down like there's no tomorrow. Why don't you wait in the car while I go and get some money."

Brick's eyes widened along with a devious grin. "Yeah, you think that might happen? I ain't that hammered."

Paco hesitated. "Don't do this on your first night out. Especially when you're this drunk."

"I need to make sure I've still got it. Ruth seems to think my time in made me soft."

"You know you've still got it. I wanted you to come along to give you time to cool down after what happened between you and Beto. I'm not going to be the one responsible for getting you locked up again the same day you got out. Macho would kill me."

Brick pushed Paco. "Screw Macho and let me worry about myself. Is that okay with you, mom?"

Paco smiled. "Yeah, yeah. I don't suppose you're giving me a say in the matter anyways."

"No, I'm not," Brick said, and held out a hand and wiggled his fingers. "Where's the toy?"

Paco's smile faded and his stare suggested he was in conflict with something.

"Give it to me," Brick said.

"Brick," Paco breathed and he watched the traffic light turn green. "This is getting serious and you've had a lot to drink."

"Now I'm no longer asking you, I'm telling. Let me see it."

"Open the glove box," Paco said.

The car behind them beeped and Brick showed them the middle finger. "Hey, screw you asshole!" He looked at Paco. "And?"

"It's in a hollow cutout behind the panel in the rear. Put your hand inside there and reach up."

Brick did, and he grabbed the handle of the gun and worked it out of the tight hiding spot. It was a Taurus .38 Special. He grabbed the stainless steel revolver, settled his hand into the rubber grip and stared down the fixed sights. "Nice gun. Where did you get it?"

"I bought it for twenty bucks off of some junky that burglarized some houses in the suburbs."

"Well something this nice deserves something a little better than a smash and grab, don't you think?"

Paco nodded. "I've done a few with it. It's quite a weapon."

"Now it's my turn. Pull down the street here and kill the engine."

Paco did as he was told. "You know," he said, "I never liked it when you got that look in your eyes. I'm seeing it right now and I know it means trouble."

Brick chuckled. "Well then, I guess it's a good thing you listened to me and I'm not after you."

Brick closed an eye and aimed the gun at Paco and then slowly moved it to a fire hydrant. He pretended it was a person cowering. He turned the gun sideways in his hand and raised his chin. "I'm going to buy the weed after we're done here," Brick said.

"You don't have to do that."

"No, I don't. But I want to as a thank you," Brick said. "You took care of everyone while I was gone and this is the least I can do for you."

"Thank you," Paco said.

Brick tapped the two-inch barrel off the dash. "No problem. That's what friends are for. Now I'll bet you some unlucky bastard that has a pocket full of change is not going to expect meeting someone like me tonight."

Brick tucked the gun into his waistband and pulled the hat off of Paco's head.

"I think it's time to do what I do best. Maybe they forgot about me. But I think I need to put a little fear into these people because I'm getting a sense that they're beginning to feel comfortable walking these streets at night. I'll be back in a minute, I have to go and deliver my first message."

He kicked the door open and stepped out into the night.

BRICK PULLED HIMSELF into the shadow of a derelict stairwell and fought against the feeling that had him numb and off-balance.

"C'mon man, get it together," he whispered to himself.

He watched a shadowy figure that appeared short, thin and feminine rounding the corner and start on the sidewalk towards him. The closer the person moved, the more details he could make out. It was a young female that had earphones in both ears and she watched the small screen with no regard to her surroundings.

"Cute, but stupid," he whispered. "Tonight I get to teach her a lesson," Brick whispered and forgot about his buzz.

Brick watched the young woman walk past him and he followed close behind, watching the way her body swayed. That was something he missed looking at, and he followed her a bit longer to capture that image.

Rushing forward, he pushed the barrel of the gun into her lower back and pulled the earphones out of her ears.

"If you make a sound, tonight is going to be the last night of your life. Do you understand me?"

The woman stiffened and dropped the music player to the ground.

"Easy," he said, and clamped his hand down on her shoulder. "Take a breath and think about what I said to you," he said, and kept her in place with ease. He twisted the gun in her back. "You know what that is, don't you?"

The woman whimpered but remained still. Her breathing was heavy and her legs shook terribly.

"That's good. Nice and easy," Brick said with an expression of pure satisfaction. "Fear can be a great thing. It can help keep you alive tonight. I promise you that what I'm after isn't worth your life."

"Please don't hurt me," she said. "Take whatever you want."

"That's a good girl and I plan on it," he said. "Now, I want you to reach into your bag and hand me your wallet over your shoulder. Make sure you don't turn around because that is a price you don't want to pay."

He listened to the woman unzip her pocketbook and shuffle through some of the items inside.

"Nothing smart," he said and dug the barrel of the gun into her side a little more. "And I don't want you speaking anymore. Just do as I say and give me what I want. If you do that, I'll leave you alone."

The woman handed him the wallet and he snatched it out of her hand. He quickly rifled through the money compartment and the sight of several twenty-dollar bills satisfied him.

"You see, this is all working out just fine," he said, and removed the bills from the wallet and stuffed them into his pocket.

"Now that you've gotten what you wanted, please just go," the woman said.

Brick threw the wallet to the ground at her feet. "And I remember telling you not to talk! Don't ever cross a Sinner," he said, and drew the weapon back and swung it into the side of her head. The loud thud of the metal hitting bone was accompanied with a spray of blood. The woman fell into a heap.

"Damn!" he said, and ran for Paco's car. "I missed that feeling!"

BRICK ENTERED THE party house with Paco and they each carried two cases of beer.

"Reserves, compliments of someone thought we were gone!" Brick shouted, and held the beer high over his head and then set them down on the floor. The crowd cheered them and he turned to the person nearest him.

"Have you seen Ruth?"

The person shrugged. "No, I haven't seen her in a while."

Brick grabbed two beers and opened one for himself. He plowed through a sea of people, spilling drinks and even knocking some people down. But no one dared to say anything.

An arm wrapped in black leather with a studded wristband reached out from the crowd and grabbed Brick's forearm, stopping him. Brick steadied himself and watched his beer.

"You're lucky you didn't make me drop my drink," Brick said, and slowly moved his gaze up the arm that held onto him. He looked into the eyes of a stranger and guzzled some beer and wiped his mouth with his sleeve.

"I'm sorry, I was just trying to get your attention."

Brick looked at the hand that still had a firm grasp on his forearm. "Is there a reason you're still touching me?"

"You were moving really fast and I was calling for you," he said, and let Brick go, raising his hands in the air. "I didn't think you heard me with all of the noise in here. I'm sorry, I didn't know how else to get your attention."

"You got it. Who are you?"

"I'm José," he said. "I'm a friend of Macho's."

"A friend, huh?" Brick studied him with obvious distrust. "If you're a friend, how is it I've never met you before?"

Although unlikely, the thought that someone might have infiltrated the gang while he was gone made him suspicious. He clenched his fist, the spot on José's chin already picked out.

"We have met before," José said. "You initiated me before you went away."

Brick stared at José with continued uncertainty. All of the alcohol he drank was interfering with his ability to think clearly.

"I've been waiting for Macho for a long time. Have you seen him?"

Brick took a step towards José, his eyes wide and intense. "Is this some sort of joke? Macho is still in prison."

"No," José said and shook his head. "Ruth called me yesterday and told me that he got out, and that he was coming here, that I was to meet him."

"Ruth called you?" he said and pulled at his chin. He took another drink and spat. "What did she say he wanted to talk to you about?"

"I don't know," José said, seeming genuinely confused. "But I just spoke to Ruth about a half hour ago. She asked if I had seen you and I told her no, that I hadn't. She told me not to tell you that I saw her and also said that Macho was supposed to be here already."

"Did she say anything else?"

José shook his head. "She just walked away."

"Really?"

"Maybe I misunderstood her."

"Maybe," Brick said and eased back on his heels.

"She was really drunk. She was slurring really bad and stumbling all over the place," José said.

"Did you see where she went?"

"That way," José pointed. "Downstairs."

"Downstairs?" Brick said and raised a brow. "Alright, I'll bite. Show me."

He tugged José's sleeve and positioned him to lead the way. Following him through the crowd and down the stairs, Brick said, "If she's not down here, that means you've been lying to me."

"She's down here," José said. "I saw her go down the stairs."

"You better hope so."

When they reached the landing, the confidence in José's voice made Brick expect to find Ruth curled up in a corner somewhere, passed out.

"Ruth?" he said into the empty black and waited for a response. When none came, he looked at José. "This is disappointing. I figured if she really wasn't down here that I would find a bunch of your friends waiting to jump me."

"I'm telling you she has to be down here," José said.

Brick went deeper into the cellar and noticed the room hooked to the left. It was much darker back there.

"See if there's a light switch for this area," he said, and listened for a moment.

José turned on the light, and it revealed a closed door set back in the rear of the room. Brick laughed at the idea that he was going to find her in a puddle of her own vomit.

"Ruth?" he said and opened the door. He was faced with the unthinkable.

The moment the cops had caught him and arrested him, they provided him with explicit details of everything he and Macho did to that guy. The cold bite of the steel cuffs that squeezed his wrists and the charges he was facing was nothing compared to the pressure he felt in his chest right now. He fought desperately to reason with what he saw, but reasoning was a skill he never possessed.

"What the hell is going on?" he said and stepped into the room.

Beto hopped off Ruth; his pants were around his ankles and his penis was erect and bulging out of his underwear.

"You've got to be kidding me!" he shouted and punched the wall.

"It's not what you think," Ruth said and moved sloppily as she struggled to pull her shirt over her head.

"Oh, it's exactly what I think!" Brick shouted. Everything was moving way faster than he could think. He looked at Beto and he was trying to get dressed. He reached for the gun he had when he went out with Paco but remembered he put it back in the hidden compartment above the glove box.

"Calm down, Brick, and let me try and explain," Ruth said.

"Shut your mouth, Ruth. You're a drunken mess and this asshole thinks it's a good idea to try and take advantage of that!"

Her hair was wild and her makeup ran down her face with the fall of tears.

"No he didn't!" Ruth shouted.

"Shut your mouth," Brick said, and tossed his beer on Ruth and threw the empty bottle at Beto.

"You are a filthy, lying bitch and nothing about you has changed! I can't believe you would do something like this. And especially with him!"

He turned around, shoved José out of the way and plodded up the stairs. Pushing his way through the crowd, he exited the house and got into Alvaro's car.

Settling behind the wheel, he punched the dashboard and screamed. He started the car.

"I should have stayed in prison," he said, and stomped on the gas pedal and dropped the transmission into drive. Tragedy reared its head and began to laugh long and hard because it knew it was on a collision course with fate.

RAINER TOOK A delicate sip of wine and placed his drink on a nearby table. He took tongs and used them to plate elegant hors d'oeuvres that consisted of potato skin curls, ham, gruye´re and honey-mustard palmiers, figs with ricotta, pistachios and honey.

Taking a bite from the ham, gruye´re and honey-mustard palmiers, he groaned in satisfaction.

As he chewed, he watched Lucas thanking a long line of people for his second chance at life. For the first time since this all began, he felt a small sense of achievement and allowed a smile.

"I saw that," Robert Cardone said from behind Rainer. He was a childhood friend and now a successful entrepreneur. They lived on Long Island when they were kids and they hung out every day until they graduated high school. "This is amazing. You should be proud."

"I am. Of everyone in here," Rainer said and he felt Robert's comment chase away his private bliss. He didn't like taking credit whether he deserved it or not.

Robert clapped Rainer's back. "You've always been so intense, Rainer. You've been like this since we were kids. I think it's okay for you to pause a moment and enjoy this victory. Life goes fast, my friend. Don't be so consumed by it that you can't even see your own successes."

"Okay," Rainer said, and laughed. "I'll do anything if it means I'll avoid getting a lecture from you."

"That a boy," Robert said, and laughed. He shared a moment of silence with his friend.

"I'm really happy for that boy. He really deserves it."

"You've given him his life back," Robert said. "And it is truly remarkable."

"Life is a precious gift."

"When I think about all you've done, I can't help but feel proud that I grew up knowing you."

"Thank you," Rainer said and smiled. "But I didn't do this on my own. There are thousands of people involved."

"To think the boy who was always picked last for games would be able to do this." Robert shook his head and Rainer gave him a gentle shove.

Robert grabbed two glasses of wine off a passing server's tray. He offered a drink to Rainer but he waved it off, pointing to a full glass of wine on the table next to them.

"Thanks, but I already have one."

Robert smiled. "Well now you have two."

Rainer took the drink and placed it next to his other one. "I suppose I do, but I have to watch myself, I'm on call."

Robert shook his head. "You left yourself on call knowing you had this event?"

Rainer nodded coolly. "I'm in service of the community."

"Well, no one could ever question your dedication to your work." He took a sip of wine. "Can you amuse me and at least hold on to one of the glasses? Maybe I'll believe you actually know how to relax."

"No, I'm good." Rainer shook his head and casually ate some more of his hors d'oeuvres.

"I'll tell you, doc, it's a good thing you use your power for the good of the people instead of the other way around."

Rainer took his glass from the table and raised it. "I can drink to that. But the people are the ones who have given me the power, just like it was them who gave it to Lucas."

Robert clanged glasses with Rainer.

"I swear," Robert said. "When you give me answers like that, I can't help but think how much you sound like a damn politician."

"Who knows, maybe that's in my future."

Robert gave Rainer a double take. "You're not considering it, are you?"

Rainer shrugged and smiled. "You never know."

"It'll corrupt you."

"Doubt it."

"It corrupts everyone."

"You think so, huh?"

"Ah," Robert said and waved him off. "You're toying with me. But I know you would win because you have the influence of ten men and they love you for who you are."

Rainer scanned the crowd to try and locate his wife. Unable to find her, he saw Stefanie talking to the fertility specialist. He raised a brow. "Now that's really good to see," Rainer said.

"What's that?" Robert said and tried to figure out what Rainer was looking at.

"Healing," Rainer said and looked at his friend. He didn't realize he said that out loud. "I like to see people healing."

"You're working again, aren't you?" Robert said.

"This is about Glenn and Stefanie."

"Things bad?"

"Worse than I thought."

"That's a shame. Your brother is a good man."

Rainer's phone vibrated on his hip. He checked it and looked at Robert.

"I'm sorry my friend, I've got to go and find Jennifer. I just got a message that a police officer from the city has been shot and I need to get to the ER."

"No problem."

"I'll speak to you during the week so we can finish our conversation."

Rainer quickly located Stefanie. "Excuse the interruption doctor," he said to the fertility specialist. "I have an emergency."

The doctor acknowledged Rainer's request with a nod and gracefully stepped away.

"Have you seen Jennifer or Glenn around?" Rainer said while he scanned the crowd.

Stefanie reached for Rainer's arm. "No, not in a while. We're all out mingling. Is everything alright?"

"I just got a message from the hospital. I have to leave immediately and prep for surgery. I should have been out the door already, but I wanted to let them know."

"You need to go," she said, practically shoving him out the door. "I'll let them know and I'll make sure Jennifer gets home safe."

"That's why I love you. Tell her I love her and I'll be home as soon as I can."

He kissed Stefanie and quickly ran to the coat check. Exiting the building, he searched his pockets for his car keys.

Once he was in his vehicle and on the road, he called specific members of his team and gave each of them explicit instructions on what he wanted ready upon his arrival. He knew his haste and their preparedness would mean the difference between the life and death of the wounded police officer.

RUTH STOOD ON her toes and shifted as she searched the crowd for Brick. The haze in the air had thickened and everything around her had become a distraction. Despite that, she saw that he was in the far end of the house, deep in conversation with Paco. She considered going to him to see whether or not he was planning on paying any attention to her, but she resisted the urge. If he missed her as much as she missed him, he would have been right there next to her, handing her the beer he promised, making up for lost time.

She sighed and retreated to the couch, plopping herself down and curling up. She felt the rejection of his affection turning to anger and contorting her face into a maddened frown. There was no way he missed her as much as she missed him. She should have trusted her feelings when she first went to see him and she should have hit him. He was a bastard and always had been. He wasn't worth her time.

"Where's Brick?" someone said from behind her, putting her anger on hold. She turned and looked at Beto.

"He should be back in a few minutes. He went off to get us some beers. I suggest you get out of here before he gets back. The time he spent in prison only seemed to make him angrier. He feels like you've betrayed the group."

"But I didn't."

"I know, but he thinks you did. There's no changing his mind."

Beto shook his head and remained silent for a moment. "He holds onto a grudge for far too long. I don't know, it almost seems like he's trying to control you."

"He doesn't try and control me. He's just looking out for me and you're jealous because you can't control me."

"I've been watching you and you've been sitting here alone for the past ten minutes waiting for him to return. You search the crowd and find him blabbing away to someone else, forgetting all about you. But regardless of what you think or hope, he hasn't changed since we were kids. No amount of time away is going to change what he is. But I think you're already starting to realize that."

"My guess is he would say the same thing about you," Ruth said.

He looked away. "I can see the disappointment Ruth."

"I'm telling you to smarten up and get away from me. He might be acting like he's changed while he was away, but I know he didn't. I see it in his eyes. If he's pushed too far, he'll turn on you worse than he already has."

Beto sat next to her. "I'm not worried about him or what he might do."

Ruth's eyes brightened, unsure if what he had said was stupid or cute. "Well, you better care."

"I don't know why you act so different when he's around," Beto said, moving even closer. "I don't know, it's like you have this really weird need to please him or something. Are you afraid of him?"

Ruth scrunched her brows. "I ain't afraid of no one, Beto. You know that. I've been raised to be the baddest bitch in town and don't you ever forget it."

"So then what do you care what he thinks, says or might do? We have the right to be happy."

Ruth stood and turned her back to Beto. "You're a sweet talker and a trouble maker. That's what you are."

"No, I'm not. I'm telling you how I feel. And just because he's out doesn't mean that's going to change my feelings."

"We discussed this already. You know that can get you hurt and we said we would keep things quiet until we could figure it out."

"I've already figured it out. I'll keep coming back until you tell me not to. But it has to be from you and you have to mean it."

"You know I can't do that," she said.

"It is stupid we even consider hiding what we have," he said, and pulled her onto his lap.

"Beto!" she said and looked at him playfully. "You really are a bad boy."

"I can be. And I know you like it."

"Are you saying these things to me because you're trying to get into my pants?"

"I meant what I said. I'll even face the big bad wolf to prove it."

"I'm drunk."

"Whether you're drunk or not, I want you every time I see you," he said, and pulled her close and kissed her. "I just wish you'd get that through your head and stop allowing the past to interfere."

Ruth eased away from the kiss and wiped her mouth. She looked in the direction she last saw Brick and she stared back at Beto with a look of marvel.

"Let's go downstairs," Beto suggested, stood and took her hand. "No one knows about it, and they don't know I live down there. We won't have to worry about him or anyone else finding us." He gave her hand a gentle tug, and she pulled away.

"You go down first. I want to make sure we're not being watched. I'll meet you in a few minutes."

"Okay," Beto said, and he quickly disappeared.

Ruth sat around for a few minutes and watched a group of girls approach and settle off to the side.

"Hey Ruth."

"José!" she said, turning around and trying to act sober.

"Do you know if Macho is here yet?"

"Not yet. Brick is around somewhere if you can find him."

"Okay. Do you know what he wanted me for?" José said.

"No, he asked that I make sure you were here. But Macho should have been here already, so just chill out until he arrives. And do me a favor and don't tell Brick you saw me. I need some time to take care of something."

"Yeah, sure," José said, and he walked away.

She watched José settle somewhere off to the side and while he wasn't looking, she slipped past the door and hurried into the basement.

"Beto?"

"I'm back here."

Moving to the back of the cellar, there was a room off to the left. When she entered, she found Beto sitting on the edge of the bed, waiting for her.

She approached him and they stood in a moment of silence filled with anticipation and nervous hearts. Ruth wanted him, always had since they were kids even in spite of the pitfalls of their past. Those things didn't matter anymore because the newness of the moment they were in was invigorating. She couldn't wait for him to do what he invited her here for any longer.

She pushed him forward and together they fell into bed with a mountain of pillows stacked around them. Throwing the pillows to the floor, she mounted him and kissed him passionately, grinding her pelvis provocatively, arousing him.

She ripped his shirt open and was bucked. Falling to her side, Beto rolled and she fell to her back. He mounted her and ground into her. She groaned and was kissed with a contagious hunger. She reached down and found Beto's button and zipper. In return her shirt was pulled opened, and she groaned in turn.

She helped to remove her shirt and pushed Beto's pants to his ankles with her feet. She reached down again to feel his excitement and what she felt didn't disappoint.

And then a sound of an uninvited intruder interrupted the moment. Ruth froze in a moment of silent contemplation and fear.

"Did you lock the door?" she said to Beto.

"You came in after me," he said.

A deep growl tensed her muscles and sent her mind on a frantic mission to find an excuse. Unfortunately, where she searched, there was no "break glass in case of emergency" sign anywhere.

"You've got to be kidding me!" Brick screamed and Beto hopped off Ruth.

"It's not what you think!" she shouted back in defense; she knew how irrational Brick could be when he was drunk.

"Oh, it's exactly what I think!"

Brick reached for something in his waistband but came up empty-handed.

"Calm down, Brick, and let me explain," she said.

"Shut your mouth, Ruth," Brick said and his anger frightened her. "You're a drunken mess and this asshole thinks it's a good idea to take advantage of that!"

"No, he didn't!"

"Shut your mouth," Brick said, and a stream of cold beer splashed her face and she couldn't believe Brick would disrespect her like that. No matter the things he had done to her, she would never stoop so low. She wiped the beer from her eyes just in time to see Brick storming off and slamming the door as he parted ways. She ran to the door, first noticing José.

"Did you tell him where I was?"

"He made me."

"Wait," Beto said and grabbed her arm. "It's okay."

"No, it's not okay," she barked, and he reared as if she had taken a bite.

"Yes, it is," he said, his voice a hopeful whisper. "Let him go and blow some steam off. It's the only way he's going to learn to accept this."

"No," she said and shook her head. "I don't like him being alone when he's like this."

"He's a big boy and has to learn how to deal with things. Shit happens."

"Have some compassion," she said, opened the door and chased after Brick.

RUTH SPILLED INTO the street as Brick raced by in Alvaro's car.

"Brick!" she screamed, but he had already turned the corner, the wheels screeching and the engine screaming as the vehicle moved out of sight.

HANGING UP HIS cell phone, Rainer pressed down on the gas pedal of his BMW V-12 760I. The vehicle catapulted him from zero to sixty miles per hour in less than six seconds. Maneuvering through traffic with the same precision he used with his scalpel, he knew every second counted to save that man's life. The operating room was already being prepped, and the only instrument that was missing was himself.

Without the warning of skidding tires or a screaming passenger, his car was slammed broadside. The impact was between the passenger door and rear quarter-panel, sending the car skidding sideways and into a utility pole. The doctor's head snapped to the side violently and his body instantly went numb. The squeal of bending steel folding all around him was deafening and he was pinned in the seat. His body was twisted in such a way that his eyes were looking at what he thought were his legs.

He cringed, knowing how grotesquely twisted they were and what that meant for him. This was bad and his legs disappeared inside the wreckage. He felt no pain and that concerned him. It was the coming comfort of shock and although he tried to fight it, it was powerful. There were so many people that depended on his health, and this particular night was no different. There was a police officer with a bunch of holes in his chest waiting for him on the operating table.

"I'm sorry," Rainer gurgled on a mouthful of blood. He spat and mindlessly continued to try and decipher what were his legs and what belonged to his car. He tried to shake his head to dislodge the confusion, but found that he couldn't move.

His body was delicately intertwined with steel, and it pinched him enough that it kept him perfectly still.

"I don't want to die," he said, his voice a raspy wheeze. "I have too much to do."

But the coming darkness descended upon him and smothered him in nothingness.

chapter 6

"MY FEET ARE killing me," Glenn said, and walked with a slight limp.

Stefanie and Jennifer laughed.

"You should try doing all of that in high heels," Stefanie said, swaying.

"No thank you," Glenn said and they got in his SUV. They were the last to leave the event, graciously standing in for Rainer in his absence.

"Is everyone buckled in?" Glenn said, and checked. "Okay, next stop, your house," he said to Jennifer.

"Alfred," Stefanie said and clapped her hands. "No stopping. Make this an easy ride. I don't want to feel the bumps!"

"As you wish," he said and looked at Stefanie and then into the mirror at Jennifer. He pretended to tip a hat.

Everyone laughed.

"I don't mean to be a buzz kill," Jennifer said. "But that boy Lucas is something else. Don't you think?"

"You can see his appreciation for life," Stefanie said.

"His smile," Jennifer shivered. "It stays with you."

"Yes, it does," Glenn agreed.

"If you think about all he's been through . . . For a boy that is only ten years old, it's amazing."

"I don't think that boy has any idea how many people he's going to influence," Stefanie said.

Glenn nodded. "When you really try and understand what he's been through, you would think he would have this profound sadness about him. But he is genuinely thankful and seems very happy in his skin. My meeting him tonight has had an amazing effect on me and made me realize that the things I've been wallowing about really are petty things."

"Aww, Glenn," Jennifer said. "You're so sweet and you're going to make me cry."

"I mean it," he said, his voice soft. "He made me see that there is a positive way of looking at something you might think is negative."

Stefanie looked at Glenn with a smile. "Oh yeah? You got all of that from a ten-year-old boy?"

"Yeah," he said and nodded. "I really did."

Jennifer reached out from the back seat and touched his shoulder. "That's amazing," she said. "You see how he's touched people beyond the disease that once defined him?"

Glenn nodded. "I do."

"He really is an amazing inspiration," Stefanie said.

"And here we go," Glenn said, and pointed at the bright break lights ahead. "Traffic! Always traffic! I just want to get home and get out of this monkey suit."

"Do you really?" Stefanie said, and winked at Glenn.

"Uh-huh," Glenn said. "Maybe you'd like to help me?"

"All right, you two," Jennifer said and covered her ears. "I don't want to hear this and I certainly don't want to see the things I am seeing inside my mind right now."

Stefanie and Glenn laughed together and he reached for her hand. They blew kisses at each other.

"Gag me," Jennifer said.

"But seriously," he said to Stefanie with a soft tone. "I want you to know that I'm really sorry about the way I've been acting lately."

"It's okay," Stefanie said.

"No, it's not okay," he said. "Please accept my apology and know that I'm going to try and do better."

She squeezed his hand. "Thank you."

Glenn slowed the car, having to yield to the cars that were stopped in front of him. He looked in his rearview mirror, and said, "You know, there should be a law against traffic jams after ten o'clock."

Jennifer laughed. "Well, get out there and start enforcing that law!"

"Yeah deputy, pull out your pistol," Stefanie said.

"Stefanie!" Jennifer said, and covered her ears. "You're a pig!"

"Oh, don't act like you're all pure," Stefanie said. "The last I heard, you didn't conceive through immaculate conception."

"You're a horn dog," Jennifer said.

"And you're a prude."

"I'm reserved, not a prude."

"Wait a minute, girls," Glenn said. "Something really bad happened here. It looks like there's been an accident."

He inched his vehicle forward, working to merge into the only remaining open lane. Lights from a dozen or more rescue vehicles could be seen.

"Oh, how awful," Stefanie said. "I hope no one got hurt."

They all tried to see around the rescue vehicles.

"I hate to say it," Glenn said, "but when these guys are out here like this, diverting traffic and trying to limit what the public can see by blocking things off with their trucks, someone is hurt really bad or possibly killed."

Collectively the group quieted and the mood turned somber. They continued to inch towards the accident scene that looked deadly tragic. A car that was on its side was mangled and glass shards covered the street. A second car was wrapped around a telephone pole and rescue workers surrounded it, working inside the wreckage.

"Oh my goodness," Stefanie said in response to the brief snapshot of the devastation. "That looked really, really bad."

A state police officer motioned the traffic onwards with a lighted stick, sending them around the scene that had multiple rescue vehicles positioned like a barricade.

"Yeah, this one is bad," Glenn said, and kissed the back of Stefanie's hand and held it tight.

"Do you need to stop and help?" she said.

"No. There's nothing I can do to help them. The men that are there will take good care of the victims."

"I don't know how you do it," Jennifer said, her tone unable to hide her anxiety.

"It is a part of the job," he said.

"I know it is. But having to face those sorts of things on a daily basis has to take its toll on you."

"It will if you don't learn how to deal with it by distancing yourself and shutting it out," he said. "When you are faced with something like what you just saw, you have to do your best to shut your emotions off so you can deal with it as effectively as possible. The decisions these men and women need to make could mean the difference between life and death."

Glenn rolled past the trooper and broke free of the traffic. He stepped on the gas and put the tragedy behind them.

MACHO ENTERED THE party house. The noise of conversation and laughter were quickly stifled. José immediately came forward. "I was told you were going to be here over an hour ago."

"I didn't realize I was on your clock," Macho said, and folded his arms across his chest, annoyed by José's words.

"And I hate to be the bearer of bad news, but your brother got into it with Beto and Ruth."

"I saw some of it," Paco said.

"Is that so?" Macho said. "What did you see?"

"Your brother stomping out the door," he slurred.

"And?"

"Ruth went after him but he had already got into a car and took off."

"Where did he go?"

Paco shrugged and staggered. "I don't know, but he was really mad. I mean pissed. I haven't seen him like that I don't think ever." He belched and almost vomited.

"So where is he?" Macho said.

"I don't know. It's like I said. He just got into a car and drove away."

Macho snapped his fingers in front of Paco's face. "Listen you drunken fool. I'm already past Brick. I'm talking about Beto. Where is he?"

Paco pointed at the back of the house. "I'm sorry, man, I had too much to drink."

"Don't think," Macho said. "You did. Where?"

"They went back there somewhere."

Macho turned his gaze in the direction Paco showed him. He rolled up his sleeves and narrowed his prison-hardened gaze. His arms were thick and covered by a sleeve of tattoos and scars.

"Go on and see if he's back there," Macho said to José. "And look at you," he said to Paco. "You're a sloppy mess and I'm embarrassed to look at you."

He tried to stand up straight. "I know, I'm sorry." He burped and swayed.

"Put your drink down. You've had enough."

Paco put his drink down.

"Is this how things were run in my absence?"

"No," Paco said.

"I hope not. I think it's time you went home," Macho said.

Paco nodded.

"You do understand that you're no good to us like that. Everyone here should know that my getting out is going to gain some attention and we should be ready for retaliation. What if we needed you?"

Paco just stood there, looking at Macho, the answer to his question a million miles away.

"Go on," Macho said. "This isn't what I wanted to see was going on while I was away."

Paco left and José returned.

"Ruth and Beto are in the back. I told them to stay put until you got there."

"Well then," Macho said with a smile and cracked his knuckles. "Why don't we get this taken care of then?" He nodded towards the back of the house.

Like a pack of wolves that gathered for the hunt and hungry for the kill, the people moved through the house, following Macho.

Ruth sat on the couch and was sobbing into her hands. Beto sat next to her and rubbed her back.

"Ruth?" Macho said.

She looked at him with puffy red eyes.

"Where did Brick go?" he asked.

As if someone had flipped the switch to a light, a smile spread about her face and she jumped to her feet. She ran forward and banged her head off his chin as she hugged him.

"My God, I can't believe you're finally here," she slurred, sounding much worse than Paco. "I almost forgot you were coming here tonight, but I'm happy now. Things can go back to the way they were."

Macho didn't hug her back. "We arranged it so I could surprise Brick, remember? We were supposed to restructure."

She nodded, seeming unsure.

"I can't find him anywhere," he said as if he were talking to a child. "Do you know where he went?"

Ruth turned away and cried again.

"I want to know what you're crying about," he said. "Did something happen between you and Beto that somehow involved Brick?"

"Let me try and explain," Beto said.

"Was I talking to you?" Macho said to Beto. "I didn't ask you anything."

"No!" Ruth shouted with clenched fists and a stomp of her foot. "I want everyone to stop blaming Beto for everything that goes wrong between me and Brick. He's the one that's having a hard time dealing with this crap, not me!"

Beto sat down and Macho eyed him. "I think you should leave," Macho said to Beto without emotion. "This is a personal matter we need to work out."

Beto stood, unwilling to meet Macho's gaze.

"You know, it's Brick's problem he can't let go of the past," Ruth said, and took Beto by the arm. "He's staying here with me. He didn't do anything wrong and I don't think he should have to go anywhere!"

Macho fixed Beto with an expectant stare. "I've been more than fair with you. Although you are a blood brother I would like back again someday, I don't need to tell you I expect the same respect in return."

"No, you don't," Beto said, and broke away from Ruth's grasp. He looked at her. "I'll see you around, okay?" He began to walk away.

"Beto," Macho said, getting his attention. "I want you to know that I'm going to talk to Brick and we're going to get past this. I was serious when I said I wanted you back in."

Beto smiled. "I appreciate that Macho. But regardless of what has happened between us, I never left. When I said it was for life, I meant it. Once a Sinner always a Sinner. Southside! I've got your back."

chapter 7

"HOW WERE THEY tonight?" Jennifer said, and counted the money she owed Amanda for babysitting.

Amanda smiled. "They were perfect as always, Mrs. Bebout. We played hide and go seek, colored and even made a batch of cookies."

Jennifer raised a brow. "Cookies, huh? I promise not to complain about the sugar. How did they turn out?"

"Really good."

She handed Amanda her pay plus a little extra.

"Thank you," Amanda said and took the money and stuffed it in her pocket. "They made sure we set aside three cookies; one for you and two for their father."

"I might have to stay a little extra at the gym, but I'll have to try one. It sounds like they worked hard on it."

"They were supposed to be hearts but they came out looking like blobs. So if they ask—"

"Hearts. Got it."

"The pictures they colored are really cute and they insisted that we place them on the table so you can use them as place mats. They don't want you making a mess."

Jennifer snorted.

"They are the sweetest little kids and I feel bad taking money to watch them."

"Don't be silly. Your time is valuable and you should be paid for it."

The doorbell rang.

"That's weird," Jennifer said and looked at her wristwatch. "Midnight is kind of late for visitors, don't you think?"

Jennifer moved to the door. "You might as well grab your things and get out while you can." She watched Amanda as she hurried off to fetch her coat. She opened the door, and to her surprise, a rotund police officer removed his hat.

"Mrs. Bebout?" he said.

The incident with the young girl earlier in the day came to mind and Jennifer felt the annoyance of Rainer going behind her back and telling his brother redden her cheeks. "Did Rainer call you and ask you to come over?"

A Crown Victoria was parked in front of her house, and the thick plume of exhaust told her the engine was still running.

"I'm Officer Buckley," he said, and stepped forward. "I work in the same precinct as Glenn and he often speaks very highly of you and your husband. May I come inside for a moment?"

"Is this about the girl today?"

"I'm sorry ma'am, I'm not really sure what you're referring to, but I'm here to inform you of a terrible accident your husband was involved in. You need to come with me to the hospital."

His words hit her like a stiff punch to the belly and she grabbed the wall, trying to steady her shaking legs.

"Ma'am?"

"I'm sorry, what did you just say?"

"Your husband has been in a terrible car crash. I've been sent here to pick you up and take you to the hospital. I've been informed that your brother-in-law was already informed and he is on his way to the hospital as we speak."

"But Rainer went into surgery. He left the fundraiser event to help someone. I think a cop was shot."

"There was an officer that was shot, but your husband never made it to the hospital."

Jennifer felt the officer's words climb up her body and grab her heart and slowly squeeze it. "This has to be some sort of mistake. My husband is a surgeon and his name is Rainer Bebout. Are you sure you have the right person?"

"I'm sorry to tell you that I'm absolutely positive," Buckley said.

Jennifer gave in to the tremble and crumbled to her knees. "I don't understand, what happened?"

Buckley helped her to stand again and he escorted her into the living room. "Is there anyone else here with you in the house?"

"Yes. My children are upstairs sleeping," she said, and nothing about the moment felt real.

Amanda came into the room wearing her coat and stopped when she saw the police officer. She looked at Jennifer. "Is everything okay?" she said.

Jennifer felt like she was boneless and was sinking into the floor. "Rainer's been in a terrible car accident. They sent this man here to take me to the hospital."

"Is he okay?" Amanda said and sat as though someone shoved her down into the chair.

"I don't think so. I'm not sure. Will you help me ready the children?" Jennifer asked. She struggled to muster the strength to try and regain her composure for the sake of her children.

"Okay, I can do that," Amanda said and stood. "No wait," she blurted. "I'll stay here and watch the children. You need to go and take care of your husband."

"IT DIDN'T HAVE anything to do with what happened earlier today, did it?"

Officer Buckley looked into his rearview mirror and saw Jennifer nervously biting her fingernails. She was staring at him. Her eyes were red and pulled wide open.

"I'm sorry?" Buckley said, confused by the question.

"What happened to Rainer," she said and pulled herself forward. She clung onto the steel cage that separated her from Buckley. "Did it have anything to do with the accident I had earlier today?"

"I'm sorry, Mrs. Bebout, but I'm not sure what accident you're referring to," Buckley said. Maybe she was in shock, he thought. She wasn't making any sense and her thoughts were scattered.

Jennifer slid back and continued working on her fingernails with aggressive biting.

"I had a lot going on," she said. Her speech was fast and barely decipherable. "The kids were starting to act up and I had to get home in time to ready myself for the fundraiser."

She sighed and rubbed her hands together while she shook her head.

"I was in a rush and I pulled into a busy intersection without looking. The squeal of the tires from the vehicle that tried to avoid me was frightening. When the silence came, I could hear and feel the terror in my chest. I had almost caused an accident. The driver of the car I cut in front of got out of her car and started screaming and yelling at me. I could understand why she was upset, but she was acting crazy and started kicking my car."

"Someone was attacking you?"

"She was trying, but I wouldn't get out of my car. That's why she was kicking dents into it."

Buckley looked at her in the rearview mirror and their eyes connected. She was serious. "Did you file a report?"

"No, I didn't," Jennifer said, her tone full of disappointment. "Tonight was a night for my husband to celebrate all of his hard work and I didn't want to ruin it because of some crazy girl. I figured no one got hurt and it was only a stupid dent. I just wanted to carry on with the night and forget everything that happened."

Buckley returned his eyes to the road. "Why do you believe this woman had anything to do with your husband's accident?"

"She threatened me," Jennifer said. "And I believed her. She scared the children half to death. Maybe this is retaliation for what I did."

Buckley rubbed his chin. "Huh."

"And there was this guy. He was a butcher or something. He came out of his store to try and diffuse the situation. But the girl reached into her coat and said something to him, backing him away."

"Did she reach for a weapon or something?"

"None that I could see. But after she left, the butcher came back and gave me the license plate number to her car. He said he recognized her as a local street thug that ran with a gang."

"Did he give you a name or anything?"

"No. He just handed me this foam plate he had written her license plate number on. I put it in the glove box."

OFFICER BUCKLEY RETRIEVED his cell phone from the center console and punched in the memorized phone number to his commanding officer. After two rings, the voice on the end crackled through, "Hello?"

"Hey Sergeant, I just dropped the doctor's wife off at the hospital," Buckley said. "Did I hear things correctly over the radio before that there was a guy beaten really bad inside a butcher shop across town?"

"Yeah. An after-hours customer found him and called it in," the voice on the other end of the phone said.

"Who is he?"

"Eddie DePina. Why, do you have something?"

"Yeah, I think there might be a connection between him and the doctor's wife. It seems she had a run-in with a gang member earlier today and he tried to intervene. I think you might want to have someone check inside the doctor's glove box for a white foam plate with a license plate number written on it. That may lead us to whoever got to this Eddie DePina guy."

GLENN STARED AT the chrome doors before him. His heart was pounding with the same fierceness a jackhammer uses to crack cement. He wiped his sweaty palms and grabbed Stefanie's hand and squeezed it dependently.

After he dropped Jennifer off, he arrived home to find a fellow officer waiting for him. He was asked to forfeit his guns and then he was informed that he needed to go to the hospital immediately, that it concerned his brother.

He knew the situation was grave, but he knew not to question the officer that had been sent for him because it was unlikely he had any information.

He had been in law enforcement long enough to know that everything that was happening was part of protocol. To have his guns taken away meant things were serious and his commanding officer was concerned about his mental state and he was taking the necessary precautions to ensure he didn't use his weapons to harm himself or others around him.

On the way to the hospital, the officer informed Glenn and Stefanie that another officer had been dispatched to pick up Jennifer. And like them, she was being brought to the hospital where the details of Rainer's condition could be learnt.

That was over thirty minutes ago and now, as the doors to the elevator began to slide open, Glenn sucked in a deep breath and searched for enough courage and strength to carry his family through the difficult time that lay ahead of them. Steadying Stefanie's trembling hand with a firm squeeze, he stepped out of the elevator and gently pulled her along.

Scanning seats inside the vast baron lounge, Glenn found Jennifer in the corner curled in a chair with a male doctor kneeling in front of her. They were talking, but her red face and flow of tears sent the message. Something terrible had happened to Rainer and it was worse than bad. His heart sank and he didn't know if he could go over there.

"Glenn," Jennifer said, and stood. Her voice sounded weak and desperate.

He forgot his trepidation and hurried to her. Her small body trembled, and feeling how frail she had already become broke his heart.

Stefanie gently inserted herself into the hug and they all cried together.

"What happened?" Glenn said.

The doctor pulled on Glenn's shoulder and led him to the other side of the lounge.

"My name is Doctor Tracey," he said.

He was a faceless man that wore a white smock and had pens sticking out of his breast pocket.

"Can you tell me what is going on?"

"I'm on your brother's team of physicians that worked with him on the Lucas boy case and I frequently assist him with the police officer gunshot unit. I don't have to tell you that this is a shock to the team. I want to let you know how hard this is for me to have to tell you the things you're about to hear."

Glenn plopped into a chair and hung his head; his legs were like rubber and his heart continued to pound hard.

"I don't think I want to hear whatever it is you have to say," Glenn said.

He'd seen this scenario played out a hundred times before and in a hundred different ways. He had seen and heard reactions that made the hair on the back of his neck stand, pulled at his heartstrings and even gave him nightmares. But this moment, what he was waiting to hear, it was daunting, like he was being ushered to the gas chamber. He now was like all of the other people he watched as they received news like this and the feeling was indescribable.

The doctor sat next to him and placed a hand on his shoulder. Glenn's whole body was numb and he couldn't feel the touch.

"I want you to keep in mind that what I'm about to tell you may be a bit premature," the doctor said. "But I like to deal with the facts as I see them. I've taken a series of x-rays of your brother and ran some CAT scans on him. The x-rays are showing me broken bones in his right arm, hip and both legs." The doctor slid to the edge of his seat and grabbed Glenn's waning attention.

"This is really hard to hear," Glenn said, and dropped his face into his hands and dug at his wet eyes with his palms.

"I understand. Your brother is not only a friend, but a mentor to many. To see him like this is like seeing Superman powerless."

Glenn blinked hard and tried to maintain his composure.

"The most severe thing the x-ray showed me was a break in the cervical portion of his spinal cord. The CAT scan revealed hemorrhaging of the brain and severe swelling."

Glenn looked at the doctor with a growing pain deep within his being that was unbearable. "I'm sorry, doctor, but what does this all mean? Give it to me straight."

The doctor pulled a sectioned model of the human spinal cord out of his pocket. He twirled it in his hands as he spoke.

"When someone suffers a spinal injury such as the one Rainer has suffered, the need of the use of a ventilating machine and twenty-four hour care is likely."

Glenn shook his head and took a moment to try and gather his thoughts. "What are you saying? Is my brother going to be a vegetable?"

"I'm sorry. I wish I could give you better news."

"Did you tell Jennifer this?"

Doctor Tracey sighed and rubbed his tired eyes. "Not in the same manner that I'm telling you. I was a bit more delicate with her. She is going to need some time to let what I've already told her sink in."

"She's stronger than you think," Glenn said, but he didn't know why. "They have two beautiful children at home that need both of their parents."

Glenn's voice quivered.

"And what about all of his patients that are depending on him? Who will care for them?" Glenn looked at the doctor for the answer, but when he didn't respond, it all became very real and he hated it.

He didn't want to be here, in this hospital. He wanted his brother to be healthy and wanted that magic pill that would make everything all right so they could all go back to their lives.

"I'm sorry," the doctor said, his eyes were soft but unyielding to the severity of his message. "It is my strong opinion that your brother is going to be a quadriplegic. He's broken his C3 vertebra."

"Can't you fix it?"

The doctor held up the model of the spine. "I want you to look at this again," the doctor said. "This is the portion of the spine representing the upper neck. This is where your brother has the break," the doctor pointed at the area. "The closer the break is to the skull, the more severe and long-lasting the effects will become. For the next day, severe swelling is going to surround the injury and is going to increase dramatically. This is going to be the most critical time for your brother because most patients that survive the first twenty-four hours can live about another ten years."

The doctor slid back in his seat and put the model into his pocket.

He clapped Glenn's shoulder. "If he comes out of this, there will be changes in the way his body functions. But I expect that after the swelling begins to subside, we will be able to tell whether or not he will be able to regain any of the lost functions. I'm hopeful—"

"Hopeful?" Glenn snapped; his lips pulled back, exposing his teeth. He sighed and battled the anger within. "I'm sorry, doctor," he said, mustering a whisper. "It's not you. It's just that hope is something I don't have right now."

Then he fell into silence. The embarrassment of having attacked someone that had his brother's best interest in mind was unthinkable.

"I understand," the doctor said. "You are grieving and there are no hard feelings. We all feel the same way."

Glenn pursed his lips and bobbed his head. "I'm angry that this happened to him. Everything in his life was going right."

"Yes, it was."

"Do you know what caused the accident?"

"The injury was sustained during a high-speed car accident and there are rumors that the other driver was drunk. Your brother had to be pried from the wreckage with the Jaws of Life."

Glenn's body shook violently. The terror his brother must have experienced while he was trapped inside the twisted metal made him stand. The feeling of needing to go, to flee and escape this moment consumed him.

"Are you okay?" the doctor said.

"Huh?" he said, not hearing the doctor. He remembered passing an accident on the way home from the event. There was no question in his mind that what he had witnessed was the rescue workers trying to get his brother out of his car. Why didn't he stop and offer to help?

"Why?" he said, but he knew the answer.

It was because his feet hurt.

"Please sit," the doctor said and gently tugged on Glenn's arm. "You're in shock and I'm concerned about you."

"I'm not a mean person," Glenn said. "But I hope the driver of that other car is either dead or he's suffering too. He chose to drive drunk and he's ruined the lives of dozens of people."

"I know he did."

"What happened to him? Is he still alive?"

The doctor studied his feet and opened his hands. "I think it best if you concentrate on your family."

"I'm a cop. I'm going to find out anyway."

"It's my understanding that he came out of the accident without a scratch."

Glenn ran stiff fingers through his hair. "Now I know how meaningless it is when I tell people how sorry I am when they face news like this."

"Please, Glenn, I urge you to concentrate on your family or this is going to eat you up from the inside out.

chapter 8

THE PHONE NEXT to Detective O'Callahan's bed rang and it pulled him from his late morning sleep. Throwing a pillow across the bed, he sat up with a sigh and grumbled his displeasure.

"Dammit, they can't even give me a few hours," he said. "Damn amateurs."

Picking up the phone, he bellowed, "Yeah, I'm listening."

"O'Callahan?"

"Yeah?" he said, the voice on the other end of the phone was familiar to him, but the lingering feeling of being ripped out of sleep floated inside his head and clouded his ability to finger who it was.

"I've got something you might find interesting."

"Buck?" O'Callahan said.

"Yeah, it's me."

"What is it? Are you at the precinct?"

"Yeah," he said, and breathed heavily into the phone. "I need you to come to the corner of Castell and Faber in a half hour. Can you do that?" His voice was being drowned out by a lot of commotion in the background.

"Hey, Buckley?" O'Callahan said.

"Yeah?"

"I worked a violent crime case last night and I didn't get home until a few hours ago."

"I know. I saw your reports."

"What I saw last night was horrible and I don't have any leads. I barely got any sleep and I'm not in the best of moods."

"So, what else is new?"

"All I'm saying is this better be good," O'Callahan said.

"I think I might've gotten a break in the case. Now get your lazy ass up and come and meet me."

"Imagine that. The errand boy of the precinct is calling me lazy." He shook his head and sighed as he stood. "I'll see you in a half hour."

"Make it fifteen minutes."

"Don't push it, Buckley. I feel like someone poured cement into my ears while I slept and it hardened in the back of my brain. I need a half hour."

He hung up the phone and stretched. Reaching for his off-duty mini Glock semiautomatic handgun, he slid it into the holster strapped around his ankle and gave it a ritualistic slap. Putting on his shoulder holster, he was ready for whatever Buckley had and wherever it would send him.

O'CALLAHAN PULLED THE lever to his directional down and guided the car into a turning lane. Pausing to wait for traffic to clear, he searched the large parking lot across the street and immediately located Buckley's car.

Pulling into the parking lot, he eased his car in a spot next to Buckley's, lining the driver's side windows so that they were adjacent. Rolling down his window, he watched Buckley take a bite from a fast food burger that dripped grease in his lap.

"Really Buckley?" O'Callahan said from behind a pair of mirrored sunglasses. He shook his head at his ex-partner's eating habits. "I keep telling you that crap is going to kill you."

Buckley smiled, his lips painted with ketchup. He showed O'Callahan the food inside his mouth, and said, "No crap. You sound like a damn broken record."

"When you say anything about a record, it makes you sound old. My advice is to get with current gadgetry." He looked away. "You're disgusting Buckley and you're going to make me puke."

"Well do it now before I hand you what I've got. The Captain will be pissed if you ruin the evidence."

"I told you that stuff you eat was going to kill you and you didn't listen. If the heart attack didn't scare you out of eating it, nothing will."

"I didn't like the streets." He held the burger up. "I figured this was the best way for me to get off of them."

"Well, congratulations. After a triple bypass and a month of physical therapy, you got the desk job you were dreaming about."

"Don't let the belly fool you. I've still got it. Here, take this," Buckley said, and handed a bag to O'Callahan. "You might find what's inside to be of use."

He took the bag and shuffled through the contents that consisted of a necktie, medical book, and an owner's manual for a car.

"Don't you think this would go a bit easier if you'd tell me what it is I'm supposed to be looking for?"

"The foam plate on the bottom," Buckley said.

O'Callahan held up the foam plate and inspected it. Dried bloody fingerprints were easy to see around sloppily scrawled numbers and letters that were easily identifiable as a license plate number.

"What you're holding there is the license plate number of the car that plowed into the good doctor's car," Buckley said. "And those bloody fingerprints aren't the good doctor's and they're not his wife's either."

"No, I couldn't imagine those were her prints unless she has thumbs like a linebacker."

"I was sent to pick up the doctor's wife last night," Buckley said, and leaned out the window. "When I told her about her husband, she immediately started talking. She asked me whether or not the accident had anything to do with a crazy kid she had almost gotten into a car accident with earlier in the day."

Buckley took a quick sip of soda and burped. Wiping his mouth with the back of his hand, he said, "I thought she was in shock because it sounded like she was rambling senselessly. But there was something about her worry when she told me that the driver of the other car was so irate that she kicked a dent into her car. She also said that a Good Samaritan had intervened and provided her with the other vehicle's license plate number. She said it was written on a foam plate and that she had placed it in the glove box."

"Imagine the chances of that. Sometimes luck breaks these sorta cases wide open."

"I heard the call come in last night just before I picked up the doctor's wife."

"He was beaten pretty bad," O'Callahan said. "The only thing I knew for sure was it had to be an attack of rage or revenge. There was no sign of forced entry, and nothing was left behind other than a huge hole in the side of his head. I mean nothing."

"What are the chances this is a coincidence?"

"Nil," O'Callahan said, and sat up tall. "Someone was very pissed off at him. I guess I should get a move on while the trail is warm."

"The Captain wants an update as soon as you have one. He doesn't want the news getting a whiff of this. The community is already showing their outrage over the doctor being injured. Wait until they find out how bad."

O'Callahan nodded. "I'll get in touch with the Captain later. I'm curious if the doctor's wife reported anything?"

Buckley shook his head and his double chin swayed. "The doctor had a fundraising event last night and she said she didn't want to lessen its importance or change the mood."

"How convenient that was for the people that beat the hell out of the butcher," O'Callahan said. "If I had a dime for every time this type of stuff could be prevented, I'd be a damn millionaire."

"Well, you know what they say about hindsight," Buckley said.

"Did you get a status on the butcher?"

"He's still alive but unconscious. When I came in this morning, I took the liberty of reading through some of the reports to see if there was anything that might have been missed. Everyone has been thorough. This butcher guy, Eddie DePina, he's been on at least two-dozen police reports involving accidents at the intersection outside his business. He's been lobbying for a traffic light, stating that the intersection is unsafe because it is busy and it is controlled by a blinking light that people seem to ignore."

"Is there anything else you can tell me that I might find useful before I go?"

"Jennifer said the driver of the car that hit her was a young female. The owner of the vehicle is a guy named Alvaro Martinez. He's a local kid that's had a few run-ins with the law and he's a known gang member. Now that we're out looking for him, he's suddenly gone."

"Well," O'Callahan said, handing the items back to Buckley. "I guess I'll start with this Alvaro Martinez guy. I'd like to see what I can come up with. Do you have an address for me?"

Buckley scribbled down the information on a napkin. "Here you go. Even though you're an ornery bastard, I want you to be careful. Something about this is looking really ugly to me."

He took the napkin. "Yeah, ugly, just like you Buckley."

O'Callahan rolled up his window and drove away.

chapter 9

O'CALLAHAN PACED THE floor of his upstairs bedroom and his mind raced and wouldn't quiet. After his meeting with Buckley, he attempted to fit in a much-needed nap. But the information he'd been handed consumed him and he needed to follow the lead.

First, he needed to formulate a plan.

"I need to do this with kid gloves," he said, and swung his arms as he continued to pace. Picking up the phone for what seemed like the hundredth time, he plopped onto the couch.

"Damn," he whispered and tapped the phone off his forehead. Pressing the talk button, he dialed Glenn's number. To his surprise, Glenn answered the phone after the first ring.

"I was wondering when the Captain was going to assign you to the case," Glenn said. His voice was hoarse and he sounded dead tired.

"How are you doing?" O'Callahan said.

"I'm tired," Glenn said. "The doctor sent us home this morning. He told us there wasn't anything we could do, that we should go and try and get some rest. I can't even sit down, let alone try and sleep."

"How is Jennifer?"

"Wiped out. She's been crying all damn night. It has been impossible to console her. Both of the women went into the bedrooms about an hour ago and I haven't heard a peep out of them."

"That's good," O'Callahan said. "That means they were able to sleep. Where are the twins?"

"We sent them to Stefanie's mother's house for the time being. We need some time to figure things out."

"I know it's tough, I'm sorry. I'm surprised you even answered the phone."

"I was hoping you were going to call. I have something that's been nagging me and it's about your son."

"No," O'Callahan said, his voice firm but gentle. He tipped the picture of his boy over, not wanting to see him sitting in the wheelchair bent and twisted. That would break his heart and crack his composure. "Your brother and his team did the best they could. They didn't perfect the operations the way they have today. It was an accident and I knew the risks."

"It cost you your son and your marriage and I'm sorry for that. I never told you that, and I should have. I could never have understood your pain and I was too busy trying to protect my family's name and my brother's reputation."

"Your brother is a good man. He's done a lot of good for the community. I know he said he learned a lot from my son."

"I know his death haunted him."

"You should take something so you can rest. Believe me, I know what it can do to you if you don't."

"I did and it hasn't done anything. I guess I'll give in to it sooner or later."

O'Callahan nodded as if Glenn could see him. "Yes, you will. Listen, if you need anything . . ."

"Nothing right now. I'm just glad you heard me out," he said, the sincerity wasn't lost in the gruff tone of his tired voice.

"I want you to know that I found out something interesting regarding the accident your brother was in."

"What sort of an explanation can be found from a drunken fool?" Glenn breathed, his anger palpable—even through the phone.

"Listen, I wrestled with the idea of whether or not I should tell you this."

"Whatever it is you have to say, I need to know," Glenn said, leaving O'Callahan with no room to stall. "Thank you for calling and giving me some closure. But don't leave me with questions. Not now. I can't live with the idea that there is something for me to know."

"I'm telling you this because maybe you know something and you can help me," O'Callahan said. "Buckley called me a little while ago and I met with him. He showed me some things that were gathered from your brother's car. One item in particular held everyone's attention. They found a foam plate that meat cutters use to place their chopped meat on before they shrink-wrap it. But this plate had a license plate number sloppily scrawled across it."

"What license plate number?"

"I hope you're sitting."

"Tell me."

"It is the same number to the car that slammed into your brother's car."

A long pause sent an uneasy silence crackling through the phone. "I don't understand? Did the guy that hit him try and leave the scene and Rainer wrote it down on whatever he could get his hands on?"

"No," O'Callahan said.

"What was it then?"

"It was a number a guy named Eddie DePina wrote down. He's the owner of a local meat shop and it is known that he witnessed a near collision earlier in the day that involved Jennifer. It was said the driver of the other car was expressing a little road rage when she kicked a few dents into the side of your brother's car."

"She?" Glenn said.

"Yes, a female driver," O'Callahan said and rubbed at his tired eyes. He wondered if he sounded tired to Glenn. "Jennifer told Buckley about this Mr. DePina on their way to the hospital last night. She thought the accident Rainer had last night had something to do with it. She said Mr. DePina saw everything and gave her the license plate number to the car that the woman was driving."

Silence trickled into the phone again, and this time the pause was so long, O'Callahan wondered if Glenn was still there.

"Are you still with me?" O'Callahan said.

"And was this road rage incident reported?" Glenn said.

"No, none of it was reported," O'Callahan said. "But the license plate was run to see if we could find out who this woman was. Instead we found out the car belongs to an Alvaro Martinez. He's a local street thug that has had a few run-ins with the law for assault, theft and burglary. He's also a known associate of the drunken guy that was driving the car that hit your brother. This has Southside Sinners written all over it."

"Why am I getting the feeling you're going to say Rainer might've been targeted as revenge?"

"It's a strong possibility that I'm not ruling out." He paused to add value to his next point. "Especially since this Eddie DePina was found nearly beaten to death last night inside his store. He was discovered right around the same time as your brother's accident."

"He was beaten for turning in a plate number?"

"I believe so. Obviously he offended someone by stepping forward and they wanted to send a message. I'm going to go poke my nose around a bit and stir the pot to see if I can find this Alvaro guy."

"I don't think it's a good idea you go at this alone. Off the record, I could come with you."

"You're too close to this," O'Callahan said. "I'm going to help bring these people to justice and I'm not going to let them run around unchecked. I have just enough anger left in me to keep me safe and scare them."

"I know those punks that run in the gang and they are ruthless bastards, O'Callahan. They are enough to give the gang task force a hard time. I'm sure I don't need to tell you how being a cop only makes you more of a target," Glenn said. "Especially once you start showing up on their turf and start asking questions."

"I need to do this to prove to your brother and myself that I forgive him without limitations. I know there's something more to this, but I'm not really sure what it is. Do you have any thoughts?"

"No," Glenn said. "I'm still struggling with the idea she didn't report the incident to the police. She could have saved lives."

"I'm sure there's a reason there. I'll call you later to see how you're doing and give you any update I might have."

"Sean?" Glenn whispered, and the name didn't roll off of his tongue easily. No one ever called O'Callahan by his first name.

"Yeah?"

"Please help me here. Why do you think she didn't call the cops to report what happened or even look to tell me?"

"Buckley told me she said she didn't want anything interfering with your brother's special night. She said it was all about him, not some punk kid. I know she didn't do that to hurt your brother."

chapter 10

OFFICER O'CALLAHAN PULLED his wallet out of an inside pocket on his sports jacket, opened it and exposed his badge as he approached a small group of thugs that were gathered on a street corner outside a bodega.

"Damn man, five-o," someone from the group said, and everyone pulled their caps down on their heads and whispered to each other.

"I'll let you guys get back to whatever it is that you were doing," O'Callahan said. "But first I want to tell you that I'm looking for a guy that I know is a friend of yours. If you protect him, I promise you that I'll take you down with him. Bad things are happening and I don't think you want to be a part of it."

He put his wallet away and took out a picture of Alvaro. He held it up and moved around, keeping the picture close to everyone's face.

"All of you here know exactly who this man is. His name is Alvaro Martinez."

The group fell silent and all eyes turned to a short muscular guy that was missing an ear.

"You," O'Callahan said. He remembered him from the files he reviewed before he came out to the streets to send the rats scurrying.

"Me?" Chico said and stepped forward.

"Yeah you. What are you deaf?"

Chico laughed. "Yeah, I get that a lot." He pulled a long drag off his cigarette and blew the smoke at O'Callahan. "This is harassment. Besides, we haven't heard from him in over a week. And even if we did, we wouldn't tell your pig ass."

"No," O'Callahan said. "I didn't expect you to. But when you flood the sewers, you'd be amazed at what comes out."

"You're on our turf, copper," someone said, and O'Callahan drew his weapon and looked at every one of them.

"Which one of you smart-asses said that?"

"If one of us says it, then we all said it," Chico said.

"Is that so?" O'Callahan said, and holstered his weapon and took out his badge. He lunged forward and went nose to nose with Chico. Pressing the badge into his cheek. "Does this look like a bagel to you?"

Chico shook his head. "No, it looks like a donut!"

O'Callahan relaxed and then chuckled. "Even though you're a bit deformed, I like you," he said, and placed a stiff jab into Chico's stomach and sent him down to one knee, gasping for air.

He took out his weapon and pointed it at everyone's face in a quick jerking motion. "You dirt bags might think you scare everyone, but I'm here to tell you that you don't scare me!" His eyes were wide and crazed. "Does anyone have anything they want to say to me?"

They all backed away.

"Good, you all are getting the message."

He removed a business card out of his pocket and dropped it on the ground in front of Chico. He continued to gasp for air.

"I'd like to keep this between me and Alvaro. But if you'd like me to include all of you, I would be more than happy to do the good citizens of this neighborhood a favor. If you were smart, one of you would pass this along to him. I'm sure he'll know exactly why I'm looking for him. I know how fast messages can move inside organizations such as this. Now smarten up and tell him he has until tomorrow morning to see me or I'll start picking apart your little group for obstruction."

O'Callahan fixed his jacket, threw a smile into his collar and casually strolled to his car.

SITTING ALONE IN a darkened room, Glenn pondered the words O'Callahan left him with. He couldn't find a plausible reason why Jennifer didn't go to the police and it nagged at him. If she had taken action right away, then his brother would be unharmed instead of lying in a bed crippled for the rest of his life. The driver of that car would have been arrested and the vehicle would have been impounded until its registered owner came to pick it up. That meant the drunk would never have been able to get behind the wheel and slam into Rainer.

The longer he mulled over the scenario and all of its possibilities, the more he couldn't help but place a large portion of the blame on Jennifer.

"Did you sleep at all?" a soft voice that came from behind Glenn asked. He turned to see Jennifer rounding the couch and settle next to him with a yawn. Her eyes were red and heavy and filled with familiar pain.

His heart thundered and his hands shook. "No," he said and wished she hadn't come anywhere near him.

"Is there any word on Rainer? Did the hospital call?" she said, and nodded at the phone on his lap.

"No," he grumbled. "Not a damn thing."

He tossed the phone onto the coffee table and could feel Jennifer's eyes on him. He looked up to meet her gaze, and she appeared so frail. It must have been from something she was trying to keep inside, something that was eating her up.

"Why?" he whispered through clenched teeth.

"What?" Jennifer said and sat back.

Glenn stared; everything he'd been feeling over the past hour finally reached its boiling point.

"Why didn't you report the incident you had with that girl?" he said.

"What girl?"

"If you would have reported it, that guy wouldn't have had access to that car and he wouldn't have been able to run into Rainer!"

"I don't even know what you're saying or why you're yelling at me!" she said and started to cry. "My husband is in the hospital and I'm upset!"

"Maybe that's because of you. I want to know why you didn't report the incident you had with that girl yesterday!"

"How did you know?"

"Why!"

"I did it for him."

"You did that for him?" He wanted to hit something. "The decisions you made caused this!"

"How dare you try and blame me for this!"

Glenn shook his head, his anger commanding. "It makes no sense why one of you didn't tell me. I could have had the situation taken care of with a simple phone call that wouldn't have interrupted any moment of your precious night!"

Jennifer hung her head, holding onto something she didn't want to say.

"I want to know why," Glenn shouted.

"Because I asked him not to! You know if we said something, it would've been eating you up inside all night! You're always so quick to puff your chest and throw the law around."

"I do that for obvious reasons, Jennifer!" Glenn clenched his fists and stomped his foot. "To avoid tragedies like this!"

"How would my telling you any of that have helped Rainer?"

"Have you listened to anything I've just said to you?"

She stared.

"The woman you nearly got into an accident with, the one that kicked your car and you failed to report, that very same car is the car that ran into Rainer!"

Jennifer stopped and looked at Glenn, her mouth a perfect circle filled with surprise and inexplicable terror. "Oh my God!" she said, and curled in the fetal position and bawled.

"What's all of the yelling about?" Stefanie said, obviously woken by all the noise. She looked at Jennifer and settled on Glenn.

Glenn turned away. "Go ahead, Jennifer. Tell her how you are responsible for killing my brother!"

He grabbed his jacket off the back of the chair and put it on. He left the house through the front door, departing with a forceful yank on the handle. The door slammed with such force, it rattled the windows in their frame and made Stefanie jump.

chapter 11

WHEN JENNIFER ARRIVED home, the big house was empty and the love that once filled the vast space was now gone. Her fairytale life was over and something horrible had taken its place. Although it was invisible, it was heavy and oppressing and she needed to escape it.

Jennifer went upstairs and sat on her bed in the master suite. She stared through tear-soaked eyes at a picture of her and Rainer. She fought the swell of emotion that stabbed at her heart and threatened to consume her.

The anguish inside reminded her how, in that moment the picture was taken, everything about her life had been a lot less complicated. Now, as she struggled with the reason why such senseless tragedies must be a part of life, what she looked at seemed as though it was a lifetime ago.

Rainer had been voted in as the lead surgeon of West Maple Hospital and to celebrate, he had taken her, Glenn and Stefanie on a cruise to the Caribbean. It was a time before the twins and at a time when her husband was able to move all of his limbs without a thought.

"I'm so sorry," she said and touched his image. "I didn't mean for this to happen to you."

It was a time when her brother-in-law held her blameless and spoke to her only in kindness.

She sobbed hard and her eyes hurt. The smile Rainer had in the photograph was something she knew he would never have again.

"Glenn is right," she said. "My inaction caused you harm. I was only trying to be protective."

Since Glenn had departed with a slam of the door, she had tried to understand why she didn't call the cops on that girl.

Because you were afraid of her. Afraid of what might happen if you did anything.

There was a deranged look in the girl's eyes that said she didn't care about anything or anyone. Jennifer wouldn't dare expose her family to that. She had seen that look before and she shivered at the memory that she had long ago put away, never to be taken out again. And now, here she was alone and vulnerable, unable to do anything but allow it to resurface. It was the same look her stepfather had when he beat her mother unconscious with furious backhands and an eventual closed fist punch to her cheek.

She witnessed these types of events for years and struggled to escape the images that assaulted her mind.

"It was that same look," she gasped. "I had to try and shield my family from that."

Suddenly, she could envision herself being able to make a stand against that which had made her so timid. She imagined getting a hold of it with both hands and squeezing it until there was nothing left of it. The "why" behind its existence didn't matter. It was the fact that it had existed in anyone at all that she despised.

"And yet the idea that I surrendered to it, turned my back on my beliefs, proves that I am no better than them," she said.

She stared at the picture for a moment more and felt her courage slip away. "That is why I didn't face it. I'm smart enough to know that I can never defeat it."

One at a time, she took an entire bottle of sleeping pills. Satisfied she would be able to escape her guilt, she opened a window and moved to the bed. There was a need to breathe the cool air.

She took her time to write everyone a personal note. Although a feeling of exhaustion attempted to pull her in, she took the time to verify that there was a note for her kids, her husband, and lastly, for Glenn and Stefanie. She arranged the papers in a neat stack, purposely placing Glenn's on top. She set them on the night table and shut the light, cocooning herself in the blanket.

"You never had a chance," she said, and rubbed her belly. "I know what I would write to you. I would tell you that I was doing you a favor by sparing you the pain of this life."

She resigned her fight against the evil she had tried to combat her entire life with kindness and waited for death's touch. She always thought she feared death because her husband saw it all the time and would share some of the things he would see with her.

"I can't get used to how awful people can be to each other," he had said to her one night. "I'm coming to understand that being mean is easy. But being nice is hard and it takes work. I want to be someone that works hard."

"You're a saint, Rainer," Jennifer whispered. "But I'm too tired to fight it. Please, don't be mad at me."

The pull of sleep tugged on her mind and took her away.

GLENN SLID HIS key into the doorknob and gave it a gentle twist. He pushed the door open and stepped into the still, dark house. He pulled off his coat and dropped it on the couch. Feeling welcome in the surrounding darkness, knowing that was what had started to fill his heart and soul in the past day.

"Are you okay?" Stefanie said from somewhere in the room.

"I guess," he said.

"Are you still angry?"

"I'm upset, not angry. There's a big difference."

"Do you want to talk about it?"

"Talk about what? Why my brother is in intensive care instead of caring for those in intensive care?"

"Sure, if you want to. Maybe it'll make you feel better."

He paused. "No thank you. There's nothing you can say that's going to make me feel better."

"Do you want to talk about what happened between you and Jennifer?"

"No. But it should have happened to her instead of him."

"Glenn . . ."

Her tone of voice shamed him.

"I didn't mean that," he said. It was amazing how quickly the change he proclaimed Lucas had inspired in him had worn off.

Stefanie stood and approached Glenn. "I'm really worried about the both of you," she whispered and wrapped her arms around his waist. "After you left, she cried and cried. I tried to calm her down, but she was hysterical. What was said?"

"Exactly what needed to be said," Glenn said, and pulled away. A surge of anger surfaced. "What do you think I should have said after what she did? She's a major part of the problem."

"I don't know. That's why I asked."

"Please stop digging around. I feel bad about what happened and I really don't need you adding to my guilt or trying to provoke me. I'm on edge and I don't know how I'm going to react."

"There are things you need to know," she said.

He sighed. "I don't want to do this. I'm tired."

"Jennifer refused to talk to me after you left and insisted I take her home. I told her no because I didn't want her to be alone. I tried to come up with a plausible reason as to what had happened between the two of you. I told her it was the stress and shock of what had happened to Rainer that brought out the anger."

"It wasn't that at all. It was what she did . . . Or more like what she didn't do."

"It didn't matter what I said to her, really, because the damage was done. She wanted to be alone, so bad that she left the house and called for a cab. I begged and pleaded with her and even offered to take her home at that point, but she was beyond hearing anything I had to say."

Stefanie took Glenn's coat and handed it to him. "I stopped by her house and pounded on the door. She wouldn't answer. I've called her a dozen times since then and she's not answering the phone. I'm concerned and I don't want her alone in that house. She's already been there for hours and I think you need to go to your brother's house and fix things between the two of you. You're going to need to lean on each other a lot in the coming months."

Glenn hesitated.

"You need to go to her."

He dug through his pocket in search of his car keys. Sifting through the keys on the ring, he stopped at the key Rainer gave him to his house. "Okay, I'll go."

"Thank you," Stefanie said.

STUDYING THE FRONT of his brother's house, Glenn tried to figure out where Jennifer might be. Uncertain because the entire house was shrouded in darkness, he rang the doorbell and heard Bach's Symphony

No. 5, Allegro con brio echo throughout the house. He smiled at the familiar tune, remembering the conversation he had with his brother the first time he heard the doorbell.

"I only used the part that rocks," Rainer said in satisfaction, almost bragging. "You know as well as I do that the whole song is music marksmanship. You should give it a listen and mature your musical palette a little."

Glenn laughed at his brother's odd attempt at humor. He could never understand how Rainer could listen to glorified elevator music.

"Keep your Bach and I'll keep my Rush."

"That guy's voice is beyond annoying I don't know how you can even listen to that screaming."

The melody faded and so did Glenn's reverie. He followed up his attempt to get Jennifer's attention by lifting the big brass knocker mounted in the center of the door and bringing it down swiftly. He could hear the heavy thud and he was convinced that would get her attention.

He paced the large stoop that accommodated a bench and two white stanchions that offered support to a large overhang.

She was taking too long and something about the eerie quiet encouraged him to ready the key and enter the house.

Offering one last attempt at getting her attention, he pounded on the door until it stung his knuckles.

"Something isn't right," he said, and unlocked the door and went inside.

"Jennifer, it's Glenn. I want to talk," he shouted, and his voice echoed around the house.

He shut the cold outside and waited for a response. Maybe she was curled up somewhere with a box of tissues and a picture of her husband cradled in her lap, reminiscing on the memories of better days.

"Jennifer, I'm coming up the stairs," he said, convinced she was in the bedroom. His reasoning told him that room was the furthest from the front door and the quietest room in the house. Often Rainer told him that he would go there after long surgeries and he would close the door and sleep undisturbed even with the twins hollering and carrying on.

Settling in the hallway before the bedroom door, he shivered. It was impossible to not notice the sudden drastic change in temperature. He could see the swirl of his breath and feel the cold penetrating his jacket.

Glenn moved his ear to the door and knocked, not wanting to startle her. "Jennifer?"

She didn't answer so he twisted the doorknob and was met with a waft of frigid air. There was a motionless lump under the bed covers.

"Jennifer!" he said and ran to her side. He tapped the lump and it felt deathly still. Pulling the covers back, he saw Jennifer curled in the fetal position, her face an awful white and her lips a deep blue. Vomit pooled around her head.

He shook her and searched for a pulse. Although it was faint, it was there. He fumbled for his phone and backed away from her, bumping the nightstand and knocking the papers and alarm clock onto the floor.

"911, what's your emergency?"

"This is Officer Glenn Bebout. I think my sister-in-law might have attempted suicide. Please send someone right away."

He blurted the address and hung up the phone. Looking at the floor, the letters that fell off the nightstand were spread out before him. The first thing he saw was one of the letters addressed to him.

chapter 12

GLENN PULLED THE window shade aside and looked outside. He listened to the phone ringing against his ear as he watched a looming, massive black cloud that lingered over his house dump a cold sprinkle of rain. The day was dull, stained by a depressing gray. The foliage was limp, appearing as if it were weeping.

"Buckley speaking," the voice on the other line said. It was barely audible over the noise that consumed the precinct.

Glenn turned his eyes away from the window but felt as though the clouds were going to follow him everywhere.

"Hey Buckley, it's Glenn. I need you to do me a favor."

"Sure, whatever you need."

Sympathy was a great way to get people to do things for you. And for Glenn, this created a momentary break in the clouds.

"I need you to look up an address for a Jan VanMol." Glenn spelled out the name. "She was the last customer in the store before Mr. DePina was attacked."

"That's the meat cutter from O'Callahan's case, right?"

"Yeah, that's him."

"I don't want to know how you obtained this information."

"That's good because I wasn't going to tell you anyway. Do you think you can get out of the precinct long enough to swing by her house and question her?"

"Yeah, I can do that."

"Maybe she'll remember some detail that might help us. That poor bastard got his brains beat in and we need to find out who did it and why."

"No problem."

"Thanks, Buckley. You're a good friend."

BUCKLEY PULLED IN front of a small white house and stalled his engine. He checked the address on the paper he held and verified the numbers on the house.

Satisfied they were a match, he kicked open his door and started up the walkway. He lifted up his pants but his stomach got in the way. Leaning heavily on the handrail, he lumbered up the steps and paused at the top to catch his breath. He looked back and stared at the three steps.

"Maybe I should listen to O'Callahan and go on a diet."

Sweat beaded his forehead and his heart pounded. He knocked on the door with three thrusts of his fist. Waiting a moment, he rang the doorbell and listened to the faint chime coming from somewhere deep within the home.

Several moments later, the door opened and a little old lady stared back at him. Her hair was white and her face was creased with deep lines. There was a slight hunch to her back and a gentle, uncontrollable shake to her hands.

"Yes, officer?" she said with a warm and welcoming smile.

"Mrs. VanMol, I'm Officer Buckley. Do you mind if I ask you a few questions?"

"Not at all," she said and held the door open. "Why don't you come inside and sit for a moment. Is everything alright?"

Buckley stepped inside the house and the aroma of something baking filled his nostrils. "Everything is just fine, Mrs. VanMol. It smells wonderful in here!"

"Why thank you," she said. "I just got done baking cookies for my grandchildren that are coming to see me tomorrow."

"Well, it smells like you're one heck of a terrific baker, Mrs. VanMol!"

"Please," she said, shuffling along behind him, "call me Granny Janny. When you call me Mrs. VanMol it makes me feel old."

Buckley smiled. She was cute and reminded him of his own mother. "Okay, Granny Janny it is."

"Please, have a seat," she said.

"Thank you," he said and sat.

"Would you like some cookies?"

"Oh, no thank you. You save those for your grandkids." He pulled out a notepad and pen.

"Well, I was in the middle of heating some water so I could have a cup of tea. Would you like one?"

"No thank you," Buckley said, but wished he had said yes to the cookies.

"Well, I'm going to have a cup if you don't mind."

"I don't mind at all."

Jan smiled.

"Do you recall your visit to the butcher shop the other night?"

Jan moved a trembling hand to her head and she scratched it. The teakettle started to whistle. "Are you talking about when I went to the supermarket?"

"No. Eddie DePina's place. He's a really big guy like me and he's a butcher."

Jan tugged at her chin. "I don't remember going to the butcher shop lately. It's really hard for me to get around so I try and do it all at once. I'm mostly in the house these days."

Buckley nodded in understanding. "Are you going to make your tea?"

"My what?"

"Your tea," Buckley said, and pointed at the kitchen. "The kettle is whistling and you said you wanted a cup of tea."

Jan looked into the kitchen. "Oh yes, silly me. My memory isn't what it used to be," she said, and removed the kettle from the flame and the whistling faded. "No worse than my hearing, I suppose." She poured a cup.

"I have a credit card receipt that showed you were there a few nights ago."

She sat down with her steaming cup of tea. "Are you sure?"

Buckley nodded. "Yes, I'm sure."

"You see, that's why I write myself a bunch of notes."

Buckley looked at the refrigerator and it was covered with a bunch of post-it notes. He looked at her and she was sipping her tea.

Her eyes seemed to focus on something that wasn't there, and then like someone had snapped their fingers and brought her back, she smiled at Buckley.

"I'm sorry, I didn't mean to be rude. Would you like a cookie? I just baked a fresh batch. My grandchildren are coming for a visit."

"No thank you," Buckley said. He closed his notepad and stood. He dropped his card on the table and pushed the chair in. "If by chance anything comes to mind, I would like you to give me a call."

"About what?" Jan said, and she walked Buckley to the door.

"Never mind. I thank you for your troubles," he said and left her house. As he walked toward his car, he called Glenn.

"Hey, it's Buck. The lead is dead. The poor lady can't remember anything from one minute to the next. She has dementia or something."

CHICO LOOKED OVER his shoulder to be sure no one was watching him. Reaching into the inside pocket of his coat, he grabbed the handle to a 9mm Alvaro had given him. He knocked on the door and checked his surroundings one more time. The neighborhood was quiet and Chico wondered how people could stand it.

Listening to the locks on the door sliding away, he watched it slowly swing open. "It must be nice to live in suburbia," he said and forced his way inside the house. "What worries could you have living here?" he said and showed the weapon to the old woman.

"Don't make a sound," he growled, and shut the door. He looked out the nearest window. "Who is in the house with you?"

"No one," the old woman said. "I'm all alone."

"Are you expecting company?"

"No one today," she said, her voice cracking. "But my family is coming tomorrow."

Chico walked around the house and shut any open blinds.

"You don't need that," the old woman said, eyeing the gun. "I'm too old to run and too tired to fight someone so young. I don't have much, but whatever you want, you can take it."

"I want you to do exactly as I say and you won't get hurt."

The old woman warbled when she walked. "I hurt every day. My body aches in ways I can't describe."

He stared at the old woman and saw the hunch that curved her back and watched her struggle with each step. He swung the gun, motioning her to the table. "Go ahead and sit," he said. "I'll be out of your house before you know it."

"I have to take the cookies out of the oven before they burn. They're for my grandchildren. When they cool, you can have some if you'd like."

"Go ahead and take them out of the oven. But don't do anything stupid."

Chico sat himself at the table and placed the gun on the placemat. He watched the old woman finish up in the kitchen and struggle to settle into the chair across from him.

"Seeing how difficult it is for you to move around is making me want to die young."

"I've lived a good life."

"I didn't. If you're questioned about the young guy you saw in the butcher shop, I would urge you to play dumb."

She paused. "Do you mind if I put on some water for tea? I always have tea in the afternoon. It seems to help calm my stomach."

"Go ahead," Chico said, and was a little disappointed this wasn't someone with a lot of fight in them. This was boring compared to most of the shakedowns he'd had to do. He enjoyed having to throw someone around and force the gun into the side of their head rather than have to endure being criticized by a kind old lady. Although he'd gotten an agreement that seemed sincere, it lacked the pleading and tears that normally went with his demands. He liked it better when they begged.

"Why do you threaten defenseless people?"

He sat back, relaxed. "I'm informing, not threatening."

The old woman stared at Chico as if she were a doctor trying to diagnose what troubles him. But her gaze settled on the disfigurement where his ear should have been.

"What are you looking at?"

"Nothing," she said, and turned away.

There was a knock at the door and Chico stood up and grabbed the old woman. He wrapped his hand around her mouth and whispered into her ear, "I asked if you were expecting someone. Why would you lie to me?"

The old woman shook her head and mumbled underneath his hand. Her eyes went wide and she looked over her shoulder at him.

Chico released his grip. "Don't you dare say a word."

He moved through the house like he was intimate with its layout and pulled back the curtain just enough to see who was at the door.

"It's the police," he said and returned to the old woman. Pressing the barrel of the gun to her head, he said, "Bang, you're dead. There is a cop at your door. I'm having a hard time with this."

The old woman struggled to find reason. "There's a cop at my door, right now? Why?"

"You tell me."

"I don't know!"

"Here is what you are going to do. I want you to answer the door and satisfy any questions he might have." Chico retreated to a closet and stepped inside. "Watch what you say because I'll be watching with the gun pointed right at him. Be smart if you don't want his blood on your hands."

He pulled the door closed to a crack and watched as the old woman interacted with the cop. Her performance was flawless, and undoubtedly convincing to the cop. When she escorted the cop to the door and let him out, he stepped out of the closet.

"Bravo. That was deserving of an Academy Award," he said and clapped. "Let's give him about a two-minute head start and I'll be out of your hair."

Chico sat at the table across from her and drummed his fingers on the wood, watching the clock.

After a few minutes of silence, Chico stood and pointed the gun at her, training it at her face. "I just wonder what the chances are that a cop shows up to question you at the same time I so happen to stop by. I wonder what you would have told him if I wasn't here?"

"Nothing," she said. "I didn't see anything and I don't know anything. His coming here is a coincidence."

"I don't like coincidences and I like loose ends even less." He squeezed the trigger and the hammer slammed down with a click. "This is your only warning. Don't cross Southside."

Putting his gun inside his jacket, he straightened his clothing and walked out of the house, using the back door.

GLENN WAS EXHAUSTED, but unlike Stefanie, he couldn't slow his mind enough to find sleep. He had settled on the couch and sat in the dark for over two hours and reflected on the past several days.

When Jennifer was transported to the hospital, she'd gone into full cardiac arrest. They were unable to revive her and she was pronounced dead before she made it to the hospital.

"How can I live with myself after all the things I said to her?"

Outside, the rain came down in buckets and thunder rumbled as if it were a chorus of angels protesting the senseless tragedy. Flickers of lightning provided a glimpse into the room. It was empty and he was all alone.

"Rainer," he whispered. His brother was a man trapped inside a broken body, unable to communicate and barely ever awake.

Though Glenn couldn't muster the courage to tell Rainer about the tragedy, he was there, next to Stefanie as she knelt beside Rainer's bed and took his hand. She lifted it, stroked it gently, held it to her cheek and cried on it.

"Rainer," she said and touched his face. That is when Glenn was convinced nothing about his brother remained. "I have to tell you something about Jennifer," Stefanie said. "She took her own life yesterday."

But a tear fell from the corner of his eye. That was it. Another part of his brother had died and he would never get him back again.

The thunder outside rumbled deep and long and made the house quiver around him.

"I know," Glenn said into the darkness. "That must be the sound emotion makes as it screams across the sky."

The thunder rumbled again, mocking him, and Glenn began to cry. His cell phone rang, playing Bach's Symphony No. 5, Allegro con brio and it interrupted his reverie. He looked at the caller ID and saw it was O'Callahan.

"Please tell me you got something?" Glenn said. A crackle of silence made him look at the phone. He pressed the receiver firmly against his ear. "Hello?"

"I think there's someone in my house," O'Callahan whispered, sobering Glenn instantly. "I stepped out of the shower and I heard a crash coming from downstairs."

"Do you have your gun?"

"No. I left it downstairs in the kitchen on top of the refrigerator."

Panic consumed Glenn and he leapt to his feet, moving fast. "Find a safe place to hide. I'm going to call you backup."

"No, don't do that," O'Callahan whispered, the calm in his voice grabbed Glenn's attention and held it firmly. "If this is who I think it is, I got this scumbag right where I want him. It's about time this punk gets taught a lesson."

Glenn's heart thundered. "What do you want me to do?"

"I want you to come over as quickly as you can. This may be the opportunity we've been waiting for. We might be able to force some answers out of this guy before we take him in."

"They took my guns," Glenn said.

"My car is open," O'Callahan said. "Go under the passenger's seat and look in the brown bag. Make sure you take the gloves out of the glove box before you touch it."

"Okay, I can do that."

"I need you to have a clear head. These guys have balls, I'll give them that," O'Callahan said. "But they're about to learn we're badder. Don't forget to wear the gloves before you touch the weapon."

Click!

O'Callahan hung up. Glenn had long ago forgotten about the bag O'Callahan had hidden away. O'Callahan and Buckley took the weapon off a second-rate drug dealer that had more lowlifes after him than cops. He had packed his little baggies of marijuana with oregano and O'Callahan had done him a favor by shutting him down and taking away the gun. It was O'Callahan's idea that they keep the gun, just in case.

Glenn looked up the stairs and everything was quiet and still.

"Sleep well," he said and rushed out into the night.

EASING OUT OF his car and shutting the door gently, Glenn used the cover of darkness to make his way over to O'Callahan's car. He breached the vehicle through the passenger side and pulled on a pair of tight-fitting gloves out of the glove box. Searching beneath the passenger seat, he easily located the ten-shot nickel-plated 25-caliber semi-automatic Smith & Wesson handgun. Checking the clip and chamber, he closed the door as quietly as possible and concealed the weapon by his side.

Moving to the rear entrance of the house, he squeezed the steel handle of the gun dependently and breathed his nerves away. These might be the guys responsible for the tragedy that took away his brother. Tonight, he might be able to exact some revenge.

His heart thundered as he moved into the darkness, sticking to cover. He swung the gun barrel, aiming at a row of trees he thought were people. Blind corners were taken slowly in case there were any bad guys lurking, and once he saw it was all clear, he moved quickly but as carefully as possible.

Too many times in his career he had known fellow officers that would run into a tense situation with haste in an attempt to try and offer help only to find themselves walking into an ambush.

"Okay," he breathed, arriving at the back door. Wiping sweat from his brow, he twisted the handle and pushed the door open. It moaned eerily. The still darkness lashed out like the snapping jaws of a ferocious rabid animal. But everything was quiet.

A distant crashing sound drew Glenn's attention and he remained firmly in place, hoping to identify what part of the house it was coming from.

Shouts of a desperate struggle mixed with the sounds of objects crashing to the floor were easily pinpointed to the room above him. He retreated into the backyard and looked at the second-story window. Projected against the drawn shade were two people tangled in a violent battle.

Reaching into the inside pocket of his jacket, Glenn pulled out his cell phone, dialed 911 and requested backup. Hanging up the phone, he tossed it aside and moved into the house. Making his way to the stairs, he charged, taking two steps at a time, feeling a sudden sense of panic, and using reckless abandon to offer O'Callahan assistance.

Thump, thump, thump!

Confused by the sound and sudden silence, Glenn ducked and paused near the top of the staircase. Trepidation over what was unidentifiable placed his heroic rescue on hold.

Thump, thump, thump!

He wanted to charge forward and scream, kick in the door, and kill the intruder. But he forced himself to think, to allow his training and experience to take over. Creeping forward, he followed the tip of his gun to the source of the threat.

Pressing his back flat against the wall, a dead silence interrupted his order and he breathed deep and counted to three.

He moved fast, breaching the door with a heavy kick to the doorknob, and he screamed, "Freeze!"

Shocked by what he saw, the gun sagged in his grip. Tables were toppled. Pictures that once hung on the wall were broken into pieces. Holes riddled the walls and a single lighted table lamp rolled into a corner and cast an eerie shadow throughout the room. The carpet beneath his feet was buckled, and in its center was O'Callahan. Naked and unmoving, the picture of his son was by his side. The silhouette of a large menacing man stood over O'Callahan and panted like a dog.

A large red puddle surrounded Sean's head, and his skull looked misshaped in the murky light. Glenn peeled his eyes away from O'Callahan and focused on the man that stood before him.

"Drop the bat," Glenn ordered.

The large man laughed. "He wanted me, he got me." The lumber rested on his shoulder.

Click!

Glenn pulled back the hammer on the gun and took aim. "This is the last time I'm going to tell you to drop the bat."

Clunk!

The bat rolled into the pool of blood that continued to grow around Sean's head. He raised his hands. "Okay, you got me, I surrender." The flash of his silver teeth reflected brightly as he smiled.

Glenn inched forward, tightening his finger around the trigger, contemplating the repercussions if he were to take the shot.

"Who would know or even care if I shot you right now? The world would be a better place without such a useless piece of shit like you!"

"I'm not afraid to die. Go ahead then," the big man said, closing his eyes.

"I should."

"Maybe you should, but you won't. You cops are cowards, always hiding behind your shields."

"You beat two unarmed men with a bat and you say we're cowards? You and all of your punk friends are the cowards."

"We're opportunists. We weed out the weak."

"I know who and what you are," Glenn said. "I've studied you all, getting to know each one of you."

"And we've been watching you. I want you to know that you were next."

"Alvaro," Glenn growled, and steadied the gun. "That man by your feet is my friend."

"Was, and he was a fighter, too. I wonder if you have as much fight as him. So why don't you put that gun down and show me what you have?"

"Because I've become the opportunist. The man you attacked in the meat shop is still alive."

"That's a pity," Alvaro said. "I knew I should've taken another couple of swings on him."

"He'll identify you and help put you away for a long time."

Alvaro shrugged. "You're sending me home to live with the wolves I hunt with."

Glenn kept a firm eye on Alvaro and reached to feel O'Callahan's neck. Unable to locate a pulse, a deep rolling growl worked its way up from the pit of his stomach and tensed his finger around the trigger. "You!" he shouted and a flash of blind rage filled his vision. He thrust the barrel of the gun forward and jabbed Alvaro in the throat.

Alvaro stumbled back and fell into a reading chair. His large body spilled onto the floor, and Glenn hovered over him panting wildly. He grabbed the back of his neck.

"Put your hands on top of your head and interlock your fingers. You're under arrest!"

Glenn looked at Sean's desecrated body. The entire side of his head had been caved in, mashed into an unrecognizable blob of pulverized bone and meat.

"Police!" someone shouted from downstairs.

"We're up here," Glenn shouted, and he hid the gun in his waistband.

Throwing one good punch into Alvaro's face before several officers burst into the room, Glenn released him and watched the officer's cuffing Alvaro, thinking how he should have pulled the trigger.

PART 2

Chapter 13

GLENN COULD SEE the fear in Hannah's eyes as she held onto his hand with a firm, dependent grip. Her little body trembled, and yet he believed she was brave for wanting to face the unknown.

He wondered how someone so young and fragile could be so defiant in the face of such tragedy. That answer was buried deep within her, put firmly into place by her parents through values and encouragement. And now it was his job to continue that and to protect them from whatever may cause them harm. They had been through enough and deserved to be happy.

"Hannah," he said gently and knelt in front of her. He smiled. "Everything is going to be okay."

Though nerves had forced her to smile, a quiet flow of tears exposed the scar this trauma had left behind. She sobbed and he pulled her close in a comforting hug.

"Everything *is* going to be okay," he said, and looked at Emily. Anger twisted her young face into something unpleasant and a swell of mixed emotions such as revenge, sympathy, hate and love pushed him around and he wanted to scream. Swallowing hard, he noticed Stefanie watching him with red, moist eyes.

"This is the first step in the healing process," Glenn said.

"I want to see him," Emily said, and walked to Glenn and held out her hand.

"I want you to know there is nothing for either one of you to be afraid of."

"I'm not afraid," Emily said.

Glenn stared at her for a moment and then looked at Hannah. "He's still your father and he loves you both very much. You need to remember that."

"What does he look like?" Emily said.

"He's different on the outside. But he's still very much the same on the inside," Glenn said.

"Is he creepy and you're not telling us?" Emily said.

"Emily!" Hannah said.

"What?"

"That's our dad!"

"I know who he is, stupid."

"Hey," Glenn said. "We don't speak to each other like that."

"She said it," Hannah said.

"Girls," Glenn said, and ran stiff fingers through his hair. "Your father is in a wheelchair. Although he can't speak, he can hear everything you're saying."

"I told you!" Emily said, and Hannah stuck out her tongue.

"He has a machine that stays with him. It makes noises but don't be afraid of it," Glenn said. "It's there to help him breathe."

The girls looked at him.

"He's not going to get any better, is he?" Emily said. "Is that why you've become so sad?"

"I pray every day that he's going to get better. And yes, I'm sad."

"I am too," Emily said, and he saw the loving child in her and knew it was in there somewhere, buried beneath heartache and confusion. He was glad to see it.

"I want you both to know how sorry I am that you have to go through this. If there was anything I could do to give you your daddy back, I would."

Steadying his hand, Glenn pressed the doorbell. The sound of Bach ringing throughout the house no longer reminded him of the conversation he had with his brother about musical tastes. Rather, it reminded him of the time he stood on this very stoop and waited for a dying woman to answer the door.

Terrible memories haunted him daily and each one attempted to push him closer to the edge he was already teetering on. An unspeakable rage stirred within and seemed to be growing. Ignoring it for the sake of the children, he believed it would eventually go away.

Glenn smelled a bouquet of flowers they had bought for the children as a gift to their father.

"Beautiful," he said, and held them out for the girls to smell.

Locks on the inside of the door slid and clicked and Glenn felt uneasy.

"You know," he said. "Your father told me he couldn't wait to see you guys."

It was a lie of course, said to provide the girls comfort. Rainer no longer had the capacity to speak.

"Hello," Rosie the nursemaid said as soon as she opened the door. She stepped aside and smiled as everyone walked inside the house.

Stefanie tended to the children and looked at Glenn. "You should go first. I'll stay out here with the girls until they're ready."

Glenn nodded. He tried to ignore the nervous thundering inside his chest and as he advanced towards the den, the sound of the ventilating machine squeezing air in and out of his brother's lungs made him pause.

"Come," Rosie said, offering Glenn her hand.

"I need a moment," he said.

"He's okay. He has no pain," Rosie said.

Glenn nodded and watched Rosie enter the den. Positioned between the two rooms and out of sight where he could take a moment to gather his nerves, he shivered at the sound of the loud hiss of the machine.

"Damn it," he said and couldn't stop his hands from shaking.

Weeks after the accident, the swelling in his brother's face, arms, and legs made him unrecognizable. His overall condition was worst-case scenario and he required care twenty-four hours a day, seven days a week. All of the doctors and nurses at West Maple Hospital that worked for Rainer had pitched in. They organized his care through donation so that Glenn and Stefanie could concentrate on caring for the children.

Forcing himself forward, he looked at his brother and what he saw made his heart ache. Rainer had gotten so thin that his bones protruded and his skin was thin and ghostly white. Any evidence of a great surgeon full of love and life had sadly departed and the only thing that remained was the approach of death slowly removing the life from his failing body.

Glenn approached Rainer with a smile, but Rainer's distant stare was a wordless cry for help that forced Glenn to his knees.

"How are you feeling today?" Glenn said, and wiped drool off of his brother's chin.

"I've brought the girls here to see you." He checked the harness system that kept Rainer's head and chest firmly against the wheelchair. Satisfied their settings were right, he moved to a chair across from him and sat. He noticed Rosie standing quietly off to the side.

"Thank you for taking such good care of him."

"He is loved," Rosie said.

"The man that hit you goes to trial today," Glenn said to Rainer. "The public outcry is overwhelming and they want to see him pay for what he did to you and your family."

A tear fell from Rainer's eye and Glenn wiped it away. "Please, try and be strong. They're going to punish this guy for what he did to you and your family. I want you to know that I'm going to be there to watch his face when the jury hands down the verdict."

A childish whimper moved Glenn's attention away from his brother. Hannah stood with Emily in the doorway. They held flowers that were split evenly between them and their eyes were bright and filled with tears. Glenn stood to offer the girls encouragement when, without warning, Hannah dropped the flowers she held and darted to her father's side.

"I want you to get better, daddy," Hannah said. "I want you to stand up right now and play with me!"

Glenn remained, his heart ripped from his chest. Hannah clawed at her father, trying to pull him out of the wheelchair.

"Hannah," Glenn croaked, and his feet were as heavy as cinderblocks. Unable to move, a surge of anger came alive and he balled his fists as he fought to move.

Hannah shook her father and his flaccid body wobbled in the harness. Spit oozed out of his mouth in thick stringy gobs.

"Why can't you stand up, daddy?" Hannah howled, and Emily went to her sister and calmly pulled on her shoulder, turning her around.

"He can't hear you, Hannah!"

"Yes, he can!"

"No he can't! Just look at him!"

Hannah did and then ran out of the room, wailing, and trampled the flowers she had dropped on the way out.

"What happened to him?" Emily said.

"He was in a bad car accident."

Emily placed her flowers on her father's lap and hurried after Hannah.

"I'm sorry," Glenn said to Rainer through clenched teeth. The thing of violence wanted to smash something.

"I'm so sorry it turned out like this," Glenn said, and relaxed his hands. He could feel the sting where his fingernails dug into his palms. "I didn't know this was how they were going to react. Please forgive me and be patient."

He hugged his brother and kissed the side of his face. He began to weep.

"I can't hold onto this secret anymore," Glenn said, and collapsed into the chair. "It has been eating me up inside ever since the night Jennifer overdosed on sleeping pills."

He reached into his pocket and pulled out the neatly folded suicide notes Jennifer had left behind.

"Please, may I have a private moment with my brother?" Glenn said to Rosie.

"Of course," she said and left the room, closing the door behind her.

"THE MORNING AFTER the accident, I had gotten a call from O'Callahan," Glenn said to Rainer. His hands were in a wrestling match with each other and his breathing was hard and shallow.

"He told me he obtained some information about the guy you had the accident with, but it goes back a little further than that. I was informed that Jennifer almost had an accident earlier in the day with a young woman that ran with a local street gang. This woman became extremely aggressive towards Jennifer. She tried getting at her, and when she couldn't, she resorted to taunting the children and repeatedly kicking the side of her car. Thankfully that was as far as it went."

Glenn opened the note Jennifer left, read some of it to himself, and placed it on his lap. He looked at the flowers that were flat and broken from being trampled and that was how he felt.

"This event with Jennifer and the children was witnessed by a local butcher shop owner named Eddie DePina. The man had been kind enough to intervene and provide Jennifer with the license plate number of the other car. He had written it on a foam plate he used to package chop meat and he unselfishly passed that information to her. Jennifer placed that information in the glove box of the car.

"The cop who was investigating your accident discovered it. It didn't raise any eyebrows and they didn't realize its importance until sometime after your accident. When Jennifer was picked up by a fellow officer named Buckley, she made mention of it and that is when they started to link the incidents. They soon discovered that the vehicle that hit you had the same plate number that was written on that foam plate."

Glenn paused. He licked his lips and drew a deep breath.

"When the vehicle plate was run, it was discovered the car was registered to a guy named Alvaro Martinez. It was quickly learned that Alvaro and the guy that hit you were best of friends and also leaders of a violent local gang called the Southside Sinners. I had a lot of run-ins with those guys and not one of them is worth a crap. They're violent, all of them, and they have no regard for life. About an hour before you had the accident, the butcher that helped Jennifer was found beaten and barely alive in his store.

"Armed with these connections, O'Callahan went out looking to question Alvaro to try and figure out who the girl was. We wanted them off the streets. But O'Callahan found out Alvaro was a hard person to track down. So he put a little pressure on him by questioning members of the Southside Sinners. O'Callahan, like the butcher shop owner, was beaten. But O'Callahan didn't survive his beating. These animals are getting so bold that they're killing cops now."

Glenn stood, and paced the floor. "They took my guns away and placed me on paid leave. I'm not sure how long the Captain is going to keep me out, but I can't sit on the sidelines while all of this is going on. So I decided to take matters into my own hands. As soon as I heard the butcher shop owner came out of his coma, I went to see him."

GLENN CONCENTRATED ON breathing through his mouth. Ever since the tragedy that changed his brother, the smell of hospitals nauseated him. The odor of pain, suffering and sickness increased his anxiety.

He approached Eddie DePina, the butcher that had helped his sister-in-law. Glenn saw that the butcher was in a full body cast. The eyes that looked back at him were being squeezed by a bloated bruised frown of discomfort and regret.

"Mr. DePina," Glenn said, and showed his badge. "I'm Detective Bebout. I'm terribly sorry about what happened to you and I'm hoping my abilities as a member of law enforcement can make the people responsible for your suffering pay for what they've done. Are there any details you can give me concerning the night you were attacked?"

Eddie swallowed hard. "I've already told the skinny blonde-haired detective everything I know. What was his name?" His lips were painfully swollen and his speech was mumbled. "Oh yeah, he said he was Detective O'Callahan."

"He came to you?"

"He's the first person I remember seeing when I opened my eyes."

"Were you able to share anything with him?"

"No. The last time I tried to help someone I ended up getting a bat upside my head. He also broke my arm, fractured both my kneecaps and banged in some ribs."

"I want you to know how very sorry I am that you've had to endure the pain you're suffering. I also want you to know that I have a personal interest in what happened to you because the woman you gave the license plate number to was my sister-in-law. She said you were very brave for coming forward, that you were the only one."

"I was being stupid. Look at me."

"I think the world could use more people like you, Mr. DePina. Her husband is my brother and he was hit later that night by that same car you wrote the plate number down for. Oddly enough, that happened the same night you were beaten. My brother, like you, is suffering terribly. But he won't ever heal, Mr. DePina, because he's paralyzed to the point of no speech and he can't even breathe on his own. His wife's name was Jennifer, and she was the woman you helped. She is dead now too. She committed suicide because she couldn't face what my brother has become."

Eddie's gaze slowly disappeared behind purple eyelids that clamped shut. "Good lord," he whispered, "You always think you have it bad until you hear about how bad someone else has it. I'm so sorry."

"I am too. For all of the victims," Glenn said, and stood beside Eddie's bed and looked down at him. "And I have come to you hoping that you would be willing to help me so no one else falls victim to these people again. If my inaction caused someone else to suffer, especially knowing what I know now, I could never live with myself. Please don't make me live with anymore regret than I already have."

Eddie swallowed hard and opened his eyes. "I'll tell you anything you need to know."

Glenn clapped Eddie's shoulder gently. "Thank you. Please tell me whatever you can remember from the beginning and try not to leave anything out—even if you think it's insignificant. Something that might not seem like anything can be a clue to catching these guys."

Eddie looked at Glenn and heaved a sigh. "I was in the store closing up for the evening when someone banged on the door. Honestly, I didn't want to be bothered so I ignored it. But the person continued to knock. I won't lie, I was a bit annoyed by it and I went to the door to tell whoever it was that I was closed for the night, to come back tomorrow. But when I got to the door, it was this little old lady. She was standing outside in the freezing cold, shivering. I remember how frail she looked, but I was more tired than sympathetic and I wanted to go home more than anything. I told her that the store was closed and she kindly pointed to the sign in my window that said I was still open. I felt like an idiot so I let her in. I mean how many years have I been running that shop, and day after day I turn that sign from open to closed without a thought? But the one day I want to go home on time, I completely forget."

"I would have let her in too."

"Well, when I finished helping her, I walked her to the door and let her out. That's when I must've forgotten about locking the door behind me because the next thing I knew, I heard the bells above my door jingling. I turned to see this young guy and he was as big as me, just standing in the store about two feet from my face, expressionless. The thing that I found strange was the bat he carried over his shoulder. I know this will sound a little strange, but I didn't feel threatened by him. I've faced things in my life that were a hell of a lot scarier than some punk wielding a club. I can remember asking him what he planned on doing with it, and though I don't remember exactly what his response was, I somehow knew he was there as payback from that girl your sister-in-law had the run in with."

Glenn shook his head in understanding while he took notes. "Let's back up a moment, Mr. DePina. The old woman, did you recognize her at all? Was she a regular customer?"

Eddie considered the question and shook his head. "No, I never saw her before and please, call me Eddie."

Glenn nodded. "Okay, Eddie, then. Do you remember how she paid you?"

Eddie paused. "By credit, I'm sure of it."

"I would like your permission to gather that information from your store without having to jump through hoops in getting a warrant. Will you consent to my doing that?"

Eddie groaned. "Please, whoever she is, she doesn't need to get dragged into this mess. She's just an old lady."

Glenn lowered his voice to a whisper. "I want you to know that anything we talk about is off the record. I never spoke to you, and I never spoke to her either. My Captain has me out of work until after the trial of the dirt bag that hit my brother. If I'm going to be honest with you, what I'm looking to do doesn't fit in the rules of the law."

"I would like nothing more than five minutes with that punk. I'd teach him a lesson he'd never forget."

"I believe you would," Glenn said. "But being you're in the condition you are in, I know this would be the best way for you to get back at him. Allow me to do that for you."

Eddie tried to smile but his bloated face was like a tight mask of pain.

"If something happens and you're questioned, I would appreciate it if you didn't offer any details about our conversation," Glenn said.

A throaty chuckle came from somewhere deep within the body cast. "What conversation?"

"So we have an agreement then?"

"Yeah," Eddie said. "We do."

A moment of silence filled the room and Glenn took advantage of the time to jot some final thoughts down before putting the pad away and standing. "Thank you for your time, Eddie. You've been very helpful and I wish you a speedy recovery." He turned and started to walk away.

"Wait! There is one more thing I didn't mention," Eddie said, stopping Glenn. "The guy had two front teeth that were made of metal. I remember how they flashed in the light when he smiled. I'll never forget them. They were blinding."

"That is all very good information. You've been a big help and I want to thank you for your cooperation."

"NO LEADS EVER came from that old woman that was in Eddie's store," Glenn said to Rainer. "Buckley said she was forgetful and seemed confused by everyday basic functions. Buckley checked on her again a few days later and she had forgotten he even stopped by. The only thing that brought Alvaro to the surface was O'Callahan's work at putting pressure on his known associates.

"I got the chance to talk to Alvaro a few days after he had been arrested for killing O'Callahan. I offered him a reduced sentence if he was willing to cooperate with us. The Southside Sinners were becoming extremely dangerous and the Captain wanted their operations interrupted at all costs, even if that meant we had to make a deal with the devil.

"Although the Captain was reluctant to call me in and send me into the interrogation room with that lowlife, he knew he had only one shot at this. I think the mindset was that I would make him the most uncomfortable because I was the one that found him moments after he beat O'Callahan's head in."

BREATHING DEEP, GLENN attempted to calm his nerves and organize the thoughts that raced through his head.

"Are you sure you don't want me to go in there with you?" Buckley said. "He's a real smart ass and he's going to test your nerves."

Glenn looked through the one-way mirror and watched Alvaro drumming his fingers on the tabletop and whistling casually. His wrists were cuffed, and he was bound to the table by a thick eyehook that the one-foot-long chain looped through.

"No, I'll be fine," he said, sure of himself and his abilities as a professional. "We're recording?"

Buckley nodded. "Every movement and every word."

"Good," Glenn said and went over his questions one last time. If he didn't get the answers he was looking for, he was told to make a deal. Although it made sense, it was still difficult. Having to offer a deal to a man that was responsible for killing a fellow officer and injuring countless others was unthinkable. He was ruthless and deserved nothing less than life in prison. But if the deal led to further arrests and disbanded the Southside Sinners, it was a smart move by the Captain.

Entering the interrogation room, he watched Alvaro as he approached the seat that was neatly tucked underneath the table. Alvaro stared at him with a smug smirk that let him know he had no regard for authority or remorse for the things he had done.

"May I?" Glenn said.

"Do what you want," Alvaro said. "Good cop, bad cop. Which one are you?"

"Very well,' he said, and pulled out the chair and sat. "I'm Detective Bebout, and I'd like to ask you a few questions."

"I know who you are," Alvaro said. "I so wish I had my chance to get to you. I know you didn't forget you were next."

"Next for what?"

"For my bat upside your pretty little head. I was going to do you the same as I did that guy in the store and your cop friend. I did him because he came into my neighborhood and threatened my friends."

"Well, I suppose I'm the lucky one then," Glenn said and worked diligently at keeping in check the desire to jump across the table and grab Alvaro by the throat and squeeze the life out of him. "Why did you attack that man in his store?"

Alvaro laughed. "So you're going to play the good cop and act like there's nothing between us? I'm good with that, but let me set the tone. I attacked him because he was like that cop friend of yours. He offended us and when that happens, I get involved. And when I do, I remove them."

Glenn leveled a stare into Alvaro's eyes and presented him with a lingering silence that was an attempt to make him feel uneasy. "You murdered a police officer in cold blood, Mr. Martinez. You're probably going to face the death penalty. If you're lucky, you're going to get a life sentence. If I were you, I'd hold real tight onto a rabbit's foot and start getting people on your side."

"I have people on my side. More than you."

"Maybe, but not the people that can help you with what you're facing."

Alvaro held out his hand and he faked a tremble. The chain rattled. "Now I'm scared." He laughed. "I'm no stranger to a cell and I'm not afraid to die."

"The people that will be looking after you are friends of the police officer you killed. How you're treated depends on your ability to cooperate with us."

Alvaro leaned back in the chair and his eyes showed no emotion.

"Do you really think I care? Say what you came to say so I can tell you to screw off."

Glenn stood and paced the floor. "How did the butcher get in your way? What did he do?"

"I've answered that question already," Alvaro said. "Are you deaf or stupid?" He shook his head. "Damn dude, I hit your pig friend in the head, not you!"

Those words stirred Glenn's anger and almost encouraged a reaction.

"It looks like you want to hit me. Go ahead," Alvaro said, and raised his chin.

"Oh, I do in the worst way," Glenn said. "But I uphold the law and I'm not a vigilante."

"It's like I said. You're a coward."

"How did the butcher get in your way?"

"I'd still like to see how tough you are without all of this," Alvaro said, and lifted his hands. The chain pulled tight.

"Did he somehow insult your girlfriend?"

"I don't have a girlfriend."

"Are you gay or something? I mean, if you are, it's no big deal."

The smirk departed. "Really, I look gay to you?"

"There was a girl reported driving your car. She was in a near collision and went on a rampage, kicking someone's car afterwards."

"No girl had my car."

"We have credible witnesses that say otherwise. One of the people that came forward just so happened to include the butcher shop owner. In case you forgot, he's the man that you so happened to beat with a bat."

"There is no girl."

"She came to you and asked you to take care of him for you, didn't she? She was annoyed that he came forward and she somehow orchestrated all of this because of that."

"I handle my business my own way. No broad tells me what to do."

"I'm not buying it. I want to know who this girl is."

Alvaro rested his head on the table. "It was your mother."

Glenn sat again and took his time in getting himself comfortable. "If you give me her name and tell me where I can find her, I can give you something in return."

Alvaro banged his head off the tabletop. "I already told you there is no girl."

"If you give us her name, I can guarantee you the death penalty will be taken off the table."

"Damn, you guys have an agenda and stick to it, don't you? I welcome death. Go ahead, put me out of my misery."

"You didn't have this cowboy attitude when you were staring down the barrel of my gun."

Alvaro sat up. "A bat versus a gun isn't a wise idea. I know my limitations."

"Suicide by cop. Why didn't you do it if you're looking to die?"

"I didn't want to give you the pleasure of taking my life. I'd rather you live with the regret of having missed that opportunity."

"Why are you protecting this girl?"

Alvaro pounded his fists on the tabletop. "Listen you worthless scumbag, there's is no girl."

Alvaro offered Glenn a defiant stare that broke down into a smile and eventually a giggle. He wiped spit from the corners of his mouth. "Southside is a way of life. You'll never break me."

"The offer is off once I walk out of here."

Glenn stood and walked to the door. He grabbed the knob and turned to Alvaro but he wasn't talking.

"I DON'T THINK I'll ever know the identity of the woman that attacked Jennifer," Glenn admitted. "And the fact that I can't get to her is killing me inside. She was the one to blame for starting all of this, not Jennifer."

Glenn stood and moved to a window. Peering outside, he saw a group of children about the same age as the twins playing a game of tag. He smiled at memories of the girls being out there, playing freely while he and his brother watched a football game on the television and the women remained in the kitchen talking the day away. It was a simple and relaxing time he had looked forward to during each holiday. But sadly those were just memories now, clouded by the stain of tragedy and what could never be again.

Lowering his chin, he looked at the worn papers he had been carrying around since the day Jennifer committed suicide. His hands trembled and his heart was pounding fiercely. He didn't want to face what he was about to share with his brother, but he knew he must.

"I've held onto these notes and carried them with me everywhere I've gone since the day I found them on the floor beside your bed. I've read them over so many times that I memorized every word. I've cried myself to sleep knowing that I am responsible for Jennifer committing suicide."

Glenn looked at Rainer. He was so feeble and helpless. His soul had been picked apart piece by piece since the day the car accident claimed his body and left a giant void that was filled with despair. It was obvious he didn't want to live, but didn't have the voice to tell anyone.

"I want to read you the letter Jennifer left for you on the nightstand. She wrote it just before she committed suicide."

Glenn shuffled through the papers and located the one addressed to Rainer.

"Dearest Rainer," he read with an uneven voice. "I am sorry I've made a conscious decision to quit on you this way. I know I promised you for better or worse, and when faced with the worst, I found I wasn't strong enough. Seeing what you're like now just kills me inside and I can't help but feel how my decision to not report the accident has played a big part in that. Knowing this, I find it unbearable to carry on. Though I know people say it is a selfish act, it is the only way I can relieve myself of the oppressive guilt that has consumed me. If it is at all possible to be forgiven for what I've decided to do, I hope to see you on the other side. From your loving wife, Jennifer."

He folded Jennifer's letter and placed it on Rainer's lap.

"I'm sorry I didn't read that to you sooner. I wrestled with the idea of when a good time would be to do this, and I came to the conclusion that today is a better day than any.

"With the trial starting today, I am confident that the man who is responsible for doing this to you is going to face a quick and just punishment. It's a time for us to put the things that cause us the most pain out in the open so we can deal with them. Then we can begin to move forward."

Rainer slouched and Glenn straightened him. He wiped his chin and kissed his brother's forehead. "I love you, Rainer, and if I could trade places with you, I would."

He exited the room.

"How are you?" Stefanie said.

Glenn nodded. "I'm surprisingly relaxed right now." He hugged her. "And I'm confident."

"I am too."

"We just had a nice talk. But I'm not sure how much of what I said he could hear."

"I believe he can hear everything we say," she said as if there was no doubt.

Glenn broke away from the hug. "I'm going to go to the courthouse now."

He dug into his pocket and found the note Jennifer had left for Stefanie. "I'm sorry for the things I put you through. I was being selfish and unkind. This is yours," he said, and handed her the folded note.

"What is this?" she said, and inspected the dirty, worn paper as if it were poisonous.

"I believe today is the day we can begin to heal as a family. I love you and look after the girls. They can use all of the love we can give them."

He kissed her and exited the house.

STEFANIE CLOSED THE bathroom door and shook as she unclenched the fist that held onto the folded piece of paper Glenn handed her. Lowering the lid on the toilet, she sat. Twirling the torn paper in her unsteady hand, her eyes grew as she noticed the ink that had begun to bleed through. Easy to recognize gentle dips and swirls of the pen made her drop the paper.

Panting, she looked at it with immeasurable fear of what it might say. Convinced Jennifer wrote it, she snatched it off the floor and started to work on opening it.

The first portion of the letter she exposed was the valedictory, signed by Jennifer. Tears filled her eyes and a crack formed in the barrier she had to construct around herself to keep her family together. She eagerly exposed the salutation that was addressed to her, and in that instant, the wall split from the top to the bottom and came tumbling down, leaving her defenseless against the wave of emotion that made her bellow.

A light knock on the bathroom door chased the growing emotion and it receded. She moved to the door, hid the letter behind her back, and cracked the door open and remained out of sight. "Yes?"

"I just wanted to make sure you were okay," Rosie said.

"Yes, I'm fine," Stefanie said, relieved it wasn't one of the girls. "Can you please look after the children? I'm going to need a few moments."

"The children are fine and they are eating their lunch. It's okay. They can't hear you. I just wanted to make sure you were okay."

"Thank you, Rosie," Stefanie said, and gently shut the door and locked it. She listened to Rosie's footsteps fade as she walked the hallway.

Sitting on the toilet again, she struggled to steady her hands. Flattening the note, she began to read it.

Stefanie,

I can't begin to express how hard this is for me to write. Through the years, you have been my shoulder, my counselor, my very best friend. I know we've leaned upon each other for advice, support and strength many times. Please try and understand that I didn't come to you on this because I felt it was something I needed to face alone. Where I am now is a very dark place and I couldn't get myself to drag you here with me. It is so horribly lonely and there is nothing I can do to escape it.

I believe in my heart that everything in this life, good or bad, happens for a reason. The difficulties you and Glenn have been

having, the struggles you have had to endure while trying to start
a family was put there for a reason beyond our understanding. Just
like the decisions I've made and the painful transformation Rainer's
undergone has intertwined our fate in such a way that it takes my
breath away. I think what I'm trying to say is that I believe you and
Glenn weren't able to have children of your own because you were
meant to take care of the girls.

You're a woman with strong moral character and conviction, and
I know you'll care for them without limitations. In closing, when
you feel the timing is right, give the girls the note I left them and let
them know how sorry I am and how much I love them. I know it is
impossible for anyone to understand the reasons why I've decided to
take my own life, but to try and make them understand would pull
them into the deep dark hole I find myself in. And that I cannot do
because I fear they would be unable to escape it.

Jennifer

Stefanie folded the note and her bottom lip quivered. There she sat,
stuck between a complete breakdown and the need to carry on for the
children.

chapter 14

"ROSIE TOOK THE children for a walk," Stefanie said and positioned Rainer in front of the television. She fixed the strap that held his head in place. "I thought we could watch this together."

She pressed and held the volume button on the remote and the voice of a young news reporter filled the room. She was a petite, blond-haired woman with a southern accent. She held a large microphone and the courthouse loomed in the background.

"And I've just gotten a report that the jury has already completed their deliberation of Brick Sigala," Linda Lou said. "For those of you who are just tuning in, Mr. Sigala is the young man that was named responsible for hitting Doctor Rainer Bebout who is most notably known for his charity work with children and wounded members of law enforcement. It is alleged that Mr. Sigala was driving drunk when the accident occurred. It is well known that he is a young man that is no stranger to trouble and is said to be a top member of the ultra-violent street gang known as the Southside Sinners. The judge has banned all media from being inside the courtroom due to the national attention this case has gotten. The community here has expressed their outrage over the generous doctor's condition through peaceful marches and a demand that gangs such as the Southside Sinners are forced to disband."

The television switched to a male news anchor with salt and pepper hair and a thick, curling mustache. He had deep lines that surrounded bright blue eyes, and a sharp chin. His name flashed on the screen: Hunter Scott.

"Can you give us a timetable on when we can expect to hear the jury's decision?"

Linda plugged her ear and the cameraman zoomed off her and panned the front of the courthouse. A heavy police presence encircled the courthouse, and dozens of reporters were scattered about, covering the story.

"Hunter, from what I understand, we can expect to hear the verdict within the hour. An inside source tells us that the prosecution team went after Mr. Sigala for driving while intoxicated and assault with a deadly weapon. On the other side of the courtroom, the defense team has presented a very interesting defense. They didn't deny their client was responsible, but rather, they pointed out that Dr. Bebout was speeding and driving erratically. They said the actions of both drivers are what contributed to the accident and therefore, each man is equally responsible."

Back in the newsroom, Hunter leaned on the desk heavily and shook his head. "Correct me if I'm wrong, Linda, but the doctor was hurrying to the hospital so he could perform surgery on a police officer that had been shot."

Linda flashed back on screen. "That is correct, Hunter. It is said the doctor was at a fundraising event in celebration of a patient that had been cured when he got the call to come in."

Hunter sat up and twirled a pen. "I can only wonder how effective of a defense that will be? Isn't time of the essence when someone has been shot and the only qualified doctor that performs the surgery is a half hour away? I would assume he would have to hurry to his destination in order to save the life of the wounded police officer."

Linda nodded and smiled. "I believe anyone with common sense would say so. But my sources say that it went well for Mr. Sigala and his defense team. There is a cloud of uncertainty on how the jury will rule."

Hunter placed the pen down. "Whatever the outcome, the doctor is one of this community's finest citizens and what happened to him is a tragedy. We'll be right back after a short break."

A commercial for sexual dysfunction came on and Stefanie muted the television. She knelt on the floor next to Rainer and took his hand. She wished with all of her might that she could hear him tell her how everything was going to be all right. But instead, she was forced to listen to the hiss of the ventilating machine that forced him to breathe. And to her, it sounded like an angry mob chanting, demanding justice.

chapter 15

GLENN DREW A deep breath and huffed as he contemplated the unexplainable events that started to take shape inside the courtroom. He paced nervously outside the courthouse. Privileged enough to have the trust of his fellow officers, he was allowed access to the back of the building, away from the big media presence and the onslaught of protesters.

A court officer that stood approximately five feet away was silent, wrapped in his own thoughts. Maybe, Glenn thought, he felt the change in the mood during the defense team's presentation. And maybe he felt the same worry that Brick actually had a chance at getting away with crippling his brother and destroying his family during the strong closing arguments of the defense team.

"Maybe," Glenn whispered. "I'm just nervous." He tried to shake it off.

The court officer looked at him but broke eye contact without saying anything.

It had been five minutes since he came outside to try and clear his head, but it felt more like an hour of torture. The jury was in deliberation and he was far too anxious to try and have a conversation with fellow officers about what the final outcome was going to be. His thoughts raced at a million miles an hour and his heart felt like it was keeping perfect pace.

"How can lawyers defend a person like that? They know he's guilty," Glenn said.

"Some people like sweeping up the trash," the court officer named Raymond said. "I see it everyday and can't understand it."

"They tried to make my brother look like he was at fault."

"They have nothing else and they're desperate."

"Hearing that was unbearable today," Glenn said, hurt.

"I don't know how you can be in the same room as that kid."

Glenn looked at Raymond and thought back to the moment in the courtroom when the defense team tried to make his brother appear to be a villain. "I just put my fingers in my ears. I didn't want this to be about my anger. I wanted it to be about justice."

"I'm sorry for what you're going through. The pictures they showed of the two cars were horrible. I can't believe that kid was able to walk away from it."

"I wish he didn't," Glenn said. "I've never felt so much hate towards someone as I do this guy. I was watching him and I swear he smiled when the prosecution was showing the wreckage."

"I saw it too."

"At least I know I'm not crazy. I hope the jury saw it too."

The radio on Raymond's hip crackled to life.

"They've reached a decision," the voice over the radio said. "Five minutes until they resume."

Raymond clicked the button on his radio. "Copy." He looked at Glenn. "We should get back inside now."

STEFANIE CHEWED HER fingernails in nervous anticipation of the coming verdict. The television coverage turned to guest speakers that had been a panel of prosecutors and defenders in an array of criminal and civil cases. Accident scene analysis experts and retired police captains were part of the debate. Each person speculated the outcome of the trial and most hypothesized that Brick would be found guilty of a felony DUI and would be forced to serve the better portion of his adult life in prison for his role in the accident. Most based their decisions on conditions and circumstances that had caused the accident. They also discussed the likelihood that Brick would face additional charges in the death of the police officer that the doctor was supposed to operate on.

The public outrage was a major topic and one of the guest speakers had said, "It's like a witch hunt in the neighborhood the doctor lives in. The local papers, news stations, and members of the community want this guy to hang for what he did. Doctor Bebout was well loved and respected, and that alone in my humble opinion, is enough to see Brick Sigala get slammed with the full force of the law. But I'm glad they selected members of the jury from people that lived outside of the community. We are still talking about the fate of a young man's life."

After that statement, Stefanie placed the television on mute and sat idle, waiting with Rainer for field reporter Linda Lou to inform the nation of the jury's verdict.

And finally, when Linda came onscreen, Stefanie fumbled for the remote and quickly turned the volume up.

"We're told the jury is entering the courtroom right now. Stay here with us as we will be the first to have that for you live the moment it becomes available."

The camera returned to the studio where Hunter sat straight-faced and at attention. "Can you tell me what the mood of the people there is like? Can you give us a feel for what the people are expecting?"

The cameraman panned the crowd cordoned off behind barricades to the right and left of the media huddle. Some people were holding signs, calling Brick a criminal, murderer and dream killer.

"Absolutely, Hunter," Linda said, off-screen. "As you can see by the signs people are holding, there seems to be a strong sense of unification within the community from the tragedy. As if in one voice, they're saying they want this guy to be held accountable for his actions and to the full extent of the law."

"Is there any word on how effective the defense team was at portraying the doctor as holding some responsibility due to his high rate of speed?" Hunter said, and the screen split between the two reporters.

"It is all just speculation at this point, Hunter, but there are rumblings that the way they presented it was damaging to the doctor and the prosecution. I think the thing that hurt the prosecution team the most came from an unnamed source. They told me that the defense team hired their own crime scene expert. It is said this expert measured the skid marks to determine how fast the doctor was going. It is speculated that he was going in excess of speeds of over eighty miles per hour in a fifty mile an hour speed zone. When they measured Mr. Sigala's skid marks, it was determined he was doing the speed limit."

Hunter offered a discontented smile and shook his head. "Has anyone thought to question where a street gang such as the Southside Sinners gets their money to pay for a defense team like this?

"That is an interesting question, Hunter. One that should be explored in further detail."

"It seems they're leaving room for these people to wiggle out of the mess they created. I think it would be fair to say that a doctor called to emergency surgery on a patient that's barely clinging to life is a necessary reason to speed."

Linda lowered her head and plugged her ear. "I'm sorry to interrupt our conversation, but my source just told me that the jury was instructed by the judge moments before they exited the courtroom that they should come to their decision by applying the law and not emotion. He said they shouldn't place the doctor or his actions above the law."

"I hate to keep going in circles about this," Hunter said, "but a police officer was shot and his life was on the line. I'm not making any accusations, but I wonder if a member of the Southside Sinners had anything to do with that shooting?"

Linda took her hand away from her ear and nodded. "That, too, is a compelling question," she said, and remained silent for a moment before she focused on the camera. "I've just received word that the jury foreperson has just delivered the verdict of a DUI misdemeanor. Mr. Sigala has been found guilty of a DUI misdemeanor and not felony DUI. Apparently the jury arrived at this decision because they found the doctor's actions to be a contributing factor in the accident."

"Although we don't know all of the details in this case," Hunter said, "I have to say that I am surprised by the outcome. I'm sure details about the case will begin to surface over the coming days."

"It will be interesting to learn exactly what evidence the defense used that was so damaging to the prosecution," Linda said. "This is no doubt a moral victory for Mr. Sigala. I'm sure they're going to take this momentum and apply it to the upcoming case concerning the officer that died as a result of the collision between Mr. Sigala and the doctor."

Hunter shuffled through the stack of papers that were in front of him. "And what are the chances they'll use the same tactics they used today?"

"It seems likely they'll look to place some of the responsibility on the doctor. It will be interesting to see how the district attorney will react to this."

Loud, distant cracking sounds that came from behind Linda shook her body and sent her scrambling off-screen. The camera went out-of-focus, but quickly zoomed in on the front of the courthouse. A struggle could be seen within the main hallway inside the courthouse.

"It sounds as though a gun was just fired inside the courthouse," Linda shouted, her fear palpable and her breathing heavy.

The reaction from the surrounding crowd was riotously loud and the cameraman remained focused on the pandemonium that continued to unravel inside the courthouse hallway.

"Everything has happened so quickly that I'm not able to tell what is going on inside. I will try and gather information and report it back to you as soon as I can."

Stefanie stood and walked to the television and dropped to her knees. She stared at the mayhem of people rushing around. Her mouth hung open and she wanted to shout her objection, but the only sound that came forth was a dry wheeze. Slapping the television screen, she forced her plea, "Please no! Glenn, tell me you weren't a part of this!"

chapter 16

GLENN STOOD AND mindlessly walked into the hallway. Nothing about the moment felt real and his thoughts were scattered. He didn't understand what just happened and how the jury could be so easy on Brick after what he did to his brother.

Buckley followed close behind and he reached for Glenn's shoulder. "Are you okay?" he said.

Glenn couldn't feel the touch. How could they give Brick a slap on the wrist, especially since his brother was slowly withering away.

"Can you stop walking away so we can talk?" Buckley said, short of breath.

The genuine concern Buckley had for Glenn escaped his notice. His focus was somewhere deep within, trying desperately to hold on to the last thread of his self-control that was being pried away by outrageous decisions.

"I'm fine," he said through clenched teeth, but he wasn't. He moved towards the rear door he was allowed access to earlier in the day. "I don't need anyone breathing down my neck right now. Give me some space and let me figure this out."

Buckley grabbed Glenn's wrist. "I think you're in shock and I don't think it's a good idea for you to be alone."

Glenn stopped and faced Buckley, his fist squeezed into a tight ball and his first thought was to smash him in the jaw. Instead, he began to weep. "I'm stunned Buck. I don't know what to think or say right now. I need a moment to sort through this. Just give me some space, please."

Buckley shook his head and released the hold he had on Glenn's wrist. "I'm not going far. I'll give you your two minutes. I'll be right here if you need me for anything." He leaned against the wall near the door.

Glenn pushed his way out of the exit, throwing the door open with a bang. With no thought on what he intended to do, he walked across the parking lot and found his car. Entering through the passenger side door, he reached his hand underneath the seat and pulled out the gun he had taken from O'Callahan's car the night Alvaro attacked him. Checking the clip and the chamber for bullets, he disengaged the safety lock and looked blankly at the courthouse.

An inner fire fueled by rage, hatred and a need for revenge came boiling up from somewhere deep and forbidden. It was that same rage that blackened his soul the night of the accident. It was the same rage of pure anger and vengeance he swore he would never let get the better of him. But it did. It surfaced and it was intense and immeasurable. It moved him to his feet and sent him into an all-out sprint towards the courthouse. There was no questioning what he was about to do. It was as if he were preprogrammed and carrying out a special mission and couldn't stop until it was complete.

Up the steps and back into the rear entrance, away from the media's eye he went, sprinting past Buckley and through metal detectors that beeped wildly. He skirted around stunned courtroom officers that began to shout and chase after him.

Making his way into the courtroom Brick occupied, Glenn ran right up to him and hit him with a stiffened shoulder, knocking him to the floor.

Bursting through the doors behind Glenn were several court officers and Buckley, but they were too late. Glenn already had the gun pressed in the center of Brick's forehead.

"You killed my brother, you son of a bitch!" Glenn screamed and pulled the trigger. Brick's head exploded in a grotesque spray of blood, bone and brain matter.

The loud pop from the bullet discharging stung Glenn's ears and yanked him out of his trance. He dropped the gun and a plume of smoke leaked from the barrel.

Buckley kicked the gun away and court officers grabbed Glenn by his shirt and ran him out of the courtroom and slammed him into a wall.

Glenn didn't offer any resistance; his job was done and he felt relief. Several more bodies slammed into him, and voices that were panic-stricken and riotous blended perfectly with the ringing in his ears.

"WATCH THE WAY you're treating him. He's one of us!" Buckley shouted. He pulled at the court officers that pinned Glenn to the wall. People were slamming into him as they tried to get at Glenn, keeping him off balance.

"I said he's a cop! What the hell is wrong with you people?" Buckley bellowed, and his words were lost in the mayhem that continued to flood the courtroom hallway. "I said to watch the way you're handling him, you sons of bitches! He's not resisting!"

Buckley gained his footing and began to pull people off Glenn. "He's a damn cop and this is the way you guys treat him? Don't you dare treat him like he's a common criminal!"

Buckley wedged himself between Glenn and the people that were holding him. "I've got him!" Buckley roared and a sudden calmness began to settle in. He assumed control over Glenn and moved him towards a room that was off the main hallway.

"Where are you taking him?" a court officer said and stood in front of Buckley. He was reaching for his cuffs.

"Not here," Buckley said and nodded towards the media and the crowd that gathered outside. All eyes were on them. "I'll do it, but I'm going to do it so he has some dignity left! Now get the hell out of my way!" he said, and moved Glenn into the room. He faced Glenn into the wall and began patting him down.

"You got anything else on you?"

Glenn shook his head. "No, I don't think so. I don't really know. What just happened?"

"The boy that had the accident with your brother is dead," Buckley said, and reached for the cuffs the court officer had ready. "You shot him."

"I did?" Glenn said, confused. "How?"

"Shh," Buckley said while he cuffed Glenn's wrists. "Don't say another word or ask any questions for your own good. You get me?"

"Yeah," Glenn said.

Buckley finished patting Glenn down and came across a note that was folded in his back pocket.

"Take it," Glenn whispered with a desperate, pleading tone.

Buckley used his girth to shield himself from the officer's eyes and quickly slipped the note into his pocket.

"We'll take care of you," Buckley said. "If you're mishandled in any way, I want you to let me know."

"I'm sorry," Glenn said. "I don't even know what happened."

"You're okay now, it's all over," Buckley said and he squeezed Glenn's shoulder.

"No," Glenn said and shook his head frantically. "You said I just killed a man, didn't you?"

"I've said too much," Buckley said. "Don't say anything more and don't ask any questions. Do you understand me?"

Glenn nodded.

"He's one of us," Buckley said and handed Glenn off to the court officer. "Make sure he's treated properly."

chapter 17

"IT HAS BEEN confirmed that only moments ago Officer Bebout, the younger brother to Doctor Rainer Bebout, came into the courtroom with a gun and shot Mr. Sigala in the head," Linda Lou said.

The courthouse was behind her and the police activity was high.

"Mr. Sigala was pronounced dead at the scene, while Officer Bebout was taken into custody. Witnesses are saying that Officer Bebout was submissive to the authorities after the shooting and that he had very little understanding of what actually happened."

Stefanie felt like her bones had become soft and someone put heavy weights in her pockets. She heaved violently and vomited. It splashed on the floor, wetting her hands, knees and television stand. Wiping her mouth with the back of her hand, she looked at Rainer with shame.

"I'm sorry," she said. "I'll clean it up."

Struggling to her feet, she went into the kitchen and gathered cleaning supplies. But before she could make it back into the room with Rainer, she dropped everything she held and collapsed to her knees and wailed in anguish.

chapter 18

STEFANIE POINTED THE remote at the television set and mindlessly flipped through all of the channels twice. She rolled to her side, shut off the television and tossed the remote somewhere in the bed beside her.

That was where Glenn slept. But lately that part of the bed remained cold and undisturbed because he was in jail. He shot and killed another man in cold blood.

"Why would you do that?" Stefanie whispered into the darkness. But the answer to that question was lost somewhere in a mind that couldn't remember large gaps of time.

"It was shock," she reasoned, and pulled the covers up to her nose. The bright illuminated numbers on the alarm clock stared at her. It was well past midnight and the stillness of the house made her uneasy. Convinced she would never be able to fall asleep again, she sat up and sighed.

It had been more than six hours since she left Rainer's house. Buckley had stopped by to pick her and the children up. He dropped the children off at Stefanie's mother's house and then he took her home.

"Glenn's going to be okay," Buckley had said.

He had been sitting with her for nearly an hour and the pity he felt for her was obvious.

"I'm worried about him," Stefanie said. "I couldn't imagine him doing something like that."

"He broke. I should've seen it in his eyes." He snapped his fingers. "The jury read the verdict and something about him changed and he didn't return until after he pulled the trigger."

To imagine it made Stefanie quiver with worry.

"But don't worry. He's going to be fine. We always take care of our own."

Stefanie questioned whether or not he was trying to reassure her or himself. He had become a good friend and she appreciated everything he had done since Rainer's accident. But this evening, she was glad Buckley left her alone because all she wanted was to be able to grieve.

But now that the crying was done, she no longer wished to be alone. The silence was deafening and she couldn't shut her mind off.

Plopping onto her back, she stared blankly at the ceiling and tried to focus on a positive moment she experienced during the day.

But strangely, a voice that was whispered and scheming sounded near. A chill raced down her spine as she questioned if she actually heard anything at all.

"I'm telling you, it was on only a second ago. I saw the light and it was coming from this room."

The voice was coming from outside her bedroom window. The proximity of the voice and the ominous words that were spoken frightened her and the skin on the back of her neck goosed. She sunk into the bed and kept her focus firmly on the window. And although nothing was visible, she heard those words and a female had spoken them. Stefanie looked at another window across her room and didn't see anything there either. Her eyes volleyed between the two windows and she saw the shadow of someone walking by cast on the drawn shades.

"This room?" she heard a voice outside say, but this time it was a man speaking. The tone of the voice made her slide out of bed and the fear that consumed her was intense and shook her entire body.

Crawling across the floor, she caught the phone chord with her foot and pulled the telephone and alarm clock off the night table. They crashed to the floor and she froze.

A moment of perfect silence lingered long enough that she breathed a sigh of relief.

"What, you don't think we can hear you scurrying around in there?" someone outside said and knocked at the window. The shadow of a man settled in the middle of the window and paralyzed her.

Searching the floor without removing her eyes from the window, Stefanie located the phone and tried to steady her hands enough to dial out.

Unsure if her trembling fingers were able to pinpoint the required three digits, she listened with relief to the operator on the other end say, "911, what is your emergency?"

"There are people outside my house trying to break in," Stefanie whispered.

"I need you to find a safe place to hide. I'm dispatching an officer, help is on the way."

Stefanie breathed deep and tried to gain control over her nerves. "I think they're trying to get inside the house. They know I'm in here."

"Stay on the phone with me and find a safe place to hide. Can you do that for me?"

"Yes," she said, and crawled into the closet and eased the door closed, leaving enough room that she had clear sight of both windows.

"Are you still with me?"

"Yes," she said, shaking.

"The police officer I've dispatched should be there momentarily," the operator said. "Be as still as you can and don't hang up."

"Okay," Stefanie breathed, her heart pounded and her mouth was dry. "I'm watching their shadows as they move around my window. They're talking but I can't hear what they're saying."

"I want you to stay hidden until the officer gets there. Don't come out if someone identifies themselves as being a police officer unless I verify that they are there."

"Okay," Stefanie said and continued to watch the figure standing in front of her window.

"Yeah, bring it here," the male outside her window said. His voice was loud and he suddenly and quickly moved away. She watched for a long moment without blinking and lowered the phone away from her ear so she could listen.

"Stay with me," the operator said and her words were barely enough to gain Stefanie's attention. She slowly raised the phone to her ear and continued to watch the window for any passing shadow.

"Are you still there?"

"Yeah, I'm here," Stefanie whispered while she listened and hoped they left. "I don't see or hear them anymore. I think they might've gone." She pushed the closet door open and stood.

"That's good. I still want you to remain where you are until I tell you the officer has arrived. At that time, I'm going to instruct you to open the door for him. Can you do that?"

"Yes," Stefanie said as she continued to search for the shadows.

In a sudden explosion of flying glass and splintering wood, the center of the window blew inwards. The shade was ripped off the wall and made way for something heavy that crashed where she was lying on her bed only moments before. It bounced slow and unstoppable, clunking loudly against her headboard and settling silently in the center of the bed, sagging the mattress under its massive weight.

Stefanie wanted to scream but covered her mouth and staggered backwards. Tripping over debris, she fell down and dropped the phone. Staring at the devastation, she knew she was exposed and in grave danger.

BUCKLEY HURRIED DOWN the walkway. He pulled the door open and entered the house. He weaved his way through a bunch of uniformed police officers and chose one. "Where is she?" he said.

A short patrolman pointed. "She's in the kitchen with Gravelin."

Buckley knew who Gravelin was. She was a police shrink and she had been assigned to evaluate Glenn after Rainer's accident.

"Thanks," Buckley said. Following the direction he was given, he moved into the kitchen. Stefanie sat at the table with a glass of water clasped in her hands. She was trembling and looked feeble. Wrapped tightly in her bathrobe, her eyes were purple and puffy and her hair was a mess.

"You okay?" he said, and went over to her. "You can't stay here alone. I want you to stay by me. Jackie would love to have you."

"I know, but I can't," Stefanie said. "But thank you. You and Jackie have been very good to me."

Buckley pulled her head into his stomach and he squeezed her tight. "You'll be safer there and we'll get these delinquents." He looked at Gravelin. "When you're done with her, I would appreciate it if you could get someone to escort her into her bedroom so she can gather some clothing."

"No problem. I'm wrapping up now and should be done in about five minutes or so."

"I appreciate that, Gravelin," Buckley said, and he went into Stefanie's bedroom. Instantly angered by what he saw, he said, "Bastards."

There was a big hunk of cement in the center of the mattress.

He returned to the room where his fellow officers were gathered.

"How many people do you think it took to lift that and throw it that distance and with such force?" he said to the short one but all eyes were on him.

"I'm not sure, but a lot."

"Yeah, I'd say a lot," Buckley said.

"Crime scene is coming. They're going to try and lift prints off of that brick and that should give us an idea."

"That's not a brick," Buckley said. "Bricks are much smaller than that and way easier to handle. That's a hunk of cement. There's a big difference."

Buckley pulled up his drooping trousers and slapped his belly twice. "I've got a gut feeling the Southside Sinners think they're untouchable. I think it's time we start sending them a message."

chapter 19

Jan VanMol was sitting in her favorite reclining chair, rocking back and forth with a gentle push from her right foot. The seat was worn and sagged on one side. The armrests were stained and a spring somewhere on the underside of the chair squeaked.

News reporter Linda Lou was on the television, and she was outside a residence with a boarded-up window and yellow crime scene tape that encircled the property. She spoke into a microphone, but Jan couldn't hear what was being said.

She stopped rocking, picked up the remote and aimed it at the television. When she pressed the volume button, nothing happened. Slapping the remote twice and giving it a shake, she tried again. Linda's voice became loud and clear.

"Members from a local street gang calling themselves the Southside Sinners are being sought for questioning," Linda said. "It is suspected they are responsible for a wave of crimes and death that date back to a motor vehicle accident between a distinguished doctor and one of the gang's top members.

"In this well-known case, the doctor had been paralyzed in the accident and the gang member that was convicted of driving drunk was unharmed."

"Isn't that a shame," Jan said. She was talking to a picture of her deceased husband. She shook her head. "The bad people always get away. This is a crazy world now. The place we knew and loved is long gone."

"The gang member that hit the doctor was given a reduced sentence," Linda said. "It is believed that this is what sent the doctor's brother, Officer Glenn Bebout, into a fit of rage. He killed the man that was driving the vehicle right inside the courtroom only a short time after the jury read their verdict.

"During that time," Linda continued, "another gang member named Alvaro Martinez had attacked a local small business owner named Eddie DePina with a baseball bat, leaving him in critical condition. Sources say Detective O'Callahan had been assigned to the case because of his no-nonsense approach. It is said that he immediately began to put pressure on the gang to try and force Alvaro to the surface. But what happened next was truly shocking. In an event that reveals just how brutal this gang is, Detective O'Callahan came face to face with Alvaro in his own home.

"It is said Alvaro used a baseball bat to attack the detective. Photos of the crime scene were obtained, but due to the graphic nature, we are unable to share them. I can tell you that it is one of the most gruesome crime scenes I have ever seen."

"Animals," Jan said, and shook her head.

An image of Alvaro was shown on the television and she stopped rocking.

The man on the television is the one she saw walking into the meat shop after she left. He was quiet and fast for a man so big. He tried to hide his face in the shadows, but she had seen enough of him to know what he looked like. She remembered how uneasy he made her feel but dismissed it because that was the way most of the younger people made her feel. The younger generation was short on respect and had no manners.

"You see what happens when you take God out of everything?" she said. "The old-fashioned way was right."

Now she understood why that kid forced his way into her house and threatened her with a gun. She was seconds ahead of the crime and they were trying to cover their trail.

She had decided to push what had happened to the side so she could enjoy her family visit. She was getting old, and year after year she would bet herself that this would be the last time she would be able to see her family. The distraction her family had provided was perfect and she hadn't taken the time to watch the news until today.

"I know if you were here, you wouldn't have allowed that nasty boy in here," she said to her husband's picture. "But I also know what you would tell me I needed to do."

She searched the archives of her mind, looking to remember the phone number and name of the police officer that had come to see her while the bad guy hid in her closet. Although she only read the business card he dropped on the table one time, she had retained the information.

She struggled to stand and walk to the phone that was on the kitchen counter. Dialing, the person on the other end answered after the third ring.

"Buckley," he said.

"Officer Buckley?" Jan said. "You were at my house a few weeks ago. You had asked me what I remembered about my time inside the butcher shop."

"Yeah," Buckley said, and Jan could tell this was something he had been waiting for.

"I have an awful lot to tell you," she said, and shuffled around the house to verify all the doors and windows were locked. "I'd like you to come over as soon as you can so we could talk."

"I'm already on my way," Buckley said.

"I'll be waiting," Jan said. "But can you call me from outside my door so I know it's you and not one of them?"

"I can do that," Buckley said, the sound of his racing engine could be heard through the phone. "I'll be there in less than five minutes."

"And not a moment longer, officer. These people are dangerous."

BUCKLEY DIALED JAN'S phone as he made his way up the walkway.

"Hello?" she said.

"I'm outside your door," Buckley said, and hung up the phone.

After a few moments, the door locks inside slid and clicked, and the door opened. "Please, come inside. You need to be more careful now too. I wouldn't be surprised if they were watching us." Jan stayed hidden behind the door.

He stepped inside the house and the door closed behind him. Jan busied herself by engaging all of the locks. When she was done, she looked at Buckley with the same gentle smile he remembered.

"I can never be too safe."

Buckley nodded his agreement.

"Now that I've called you, I'm going to need someone to watch over me," she said.

"I understand and I can help."

"They are dangerous."

"Very," Buckley said.

"I don't know if you know how dangerous."

He watched Jan shuffle to the same table and sit in the same chair she sat in a few weeks ago.

"I'm trying to do what I know is right," she said. "My husband Arthur hasn't been here for over ten years to watch over me, God rest his soul. And being alone can be worrisome."

"I know it can and I'm sorry," Buckley said. "But I can give you the protection you need."

"I believe you will," Jan said and reached across the table to touch his hand. Her skin was thin and dotted with age spots. "That day you came here to question me, one of them was here, inside my home and watching us talk. I'm sorry I had to pretend I was forgetful. I did that to protect you."

Buckley's blood boiled.

"He arrived about ten minutes before you did and he had a gun. He threatened me and told me to forget that I ever saw his friend at the butcher shop. I didn't know why he was telling me that."

Buckley looked over Jan's shoulder and saw the closet. "He was there," he said and pointed. "Wasn't he?"

Jan nodded. "He ran to the window and pulled the shade back a crack. He immediately identified you as a cop."

Buckley smiled. "That means I've arrested him before. He knows who I am."

"That is when he hid inside the closet, keeping it open just enough to watch us."

Buckley felt his cheeks getting hot. He was much smarter than these punks and they had fooled him.

"After you left, he waited a few minutes before he took your card off the table and promised harm would come to me and my family if they ever found out I said anything."

Buckley shook his head. "They're not going to be able to get within a city block of you!" Buckley's tone was snapping and strong. "Do you think you'd be able to identify this guy?"

Jan smiled. "Well, age may have taken its toll on my body, Mr. Buckley, but it has been quite kind to my mind. I've always had a photographic memory since I was a kid. In fact, I had looked at your business card only one time when you placed it on the table and I remembered all of your information."

Buckley smiled and rubbed her hand. "You are an angel that just fell into my lap."

"I'm sorry I had to fool you."

"I'm glad you did. Would you be willing to come to the precinct to try and identify this creep?"

"Absolutely. What these kids are doing is terrible and they need to be stood up to. And the one that was here threatening me? He was missing an ear and had a look about him. He was evil."

"They're making it easy for us," Buckley said, stood, and walked around the table to help Jan to her feet.

JAN SAT ON a hard steel chair that chilled her backside and exacerbated the pain she had in her lower back. She missed her chair and the way it fit her body.

"Here you go," Buckley said, and placed some books down in front of her. "I want you to take your time looking through these. If you find the person that was inside your home and you're absolutely sure about it, let me know."

Buckley settled in the seat across from Jan and she looked through the pages one at a time, scanning the faces with certain determination.

"This is him," Jan said after looking for several minutes. "He may have had both ears in this photograph, but I could never forget his face."

She tapped her pointer finger on Chico's mug shot.

Buckley looked. "Are you sure?"

Jan nodded. "I'm positive. He pointed a gun at me. I'll never forget his face."

Buckley clapped Jan's back gently and pulled her close. "Thank you, Jan. Now I can start picking these guys apart."

chapter 20

BUCKLEY PRESSED THE button on his radio.

"The subject has entered the bodega with two other members of the Southside Sinners. We are to assume they are armed and dangerous. I want everyone to wait until I give the command to move in."

He released the button and listened to the crackle of the radio. Somehow that reminded him of the shot Glenn fired into Brick's head. He was troubled by the thought of how things would have been different if he would have stayed with Glenn when he let him outside the courthouse rather than letting him go alone.

"Standing by," a voice said through the radio, refocusing Buckley's attention.

LINDA LOU STOOD in front of the camera that brought a live feed to nearly every television set in the community and throughout the nation. The courthouse was in the background and a crowd of people was off-camera, chanting their support for Glenn.

"The last time I stood in this very spot," Linda said while stepping towards the camera, "I was the first to report the shocking verdict that outraged this community. It was a tragic case where a troubled young man made a terrible decision to drink and drive. The end result was a car wreck that left a well-respected and often-celebrated doctor paralyzed from head to toe.

"Some say Mr. Sigala, the troubled young man, had gotten away with a slap on the wrist when the jury found him guilty of a misdemeanor DUI. As shocking as it was to almost every member of this community, no one was beside themselves more than Officer Glenn Bebout. He is the younger brother of the paralyzed doctor. After the jury read the verdict, it is alleged that he had walked out of the courthouse and went straight to his car where he retrieved a hidden weapon. He returned to the courthouse with a lust for revenge that left one man dead and another man's life hanging in the balance. Today we will learn the fate of Officer Bebout for killing Mr. Sigala.

"Events that soon followed the murder of Brick Sigala shocked everyone. The district attorney has charged Officer Bebout with premeditated murder and the state is seeking the death penalty.

"The DA defended his charge by stating Mr. Bebout had planted the gun inside his car in case such a verdict came in. He said he could prove it and would do so inside the courthouse behind me."

A growing chant of the people calling for Officer Bebout's acquittal distracted Linda. She plugged her ear with her finger, nodded her head, and looked at the camera.

"I've just gotten word that the verdict has been reached and the jury is on their way back inside the courtroom now."

BUCKLEY WATCHED CHICO talking to another gang member named Paco. They were big kids and Buckley couldn't wait to prove he was bigger. He played out the moment in his mind's eye, visualizing the battle. When he tossed both of them to the ground, he would kneel on the back of their necks and he would put a little extra weight to add some much-needed pain for the hell these guys had put his friends through.

"And Granny Janny," he said, looking at Chico. "Tough guy threatening an old lady."

He watched the subjects closely and they remained outside the bodega, taking puffs from cigarettes and carrying on with a conversation that had them very animated. Their arms flailed and they laughed, oblivious to what sat in wait, ready to strike.

"Laugh it up, boys," Buckley muttered, and watched another car pull up. He sat up and tried to see who was inside, hoping it was the female that started this all because of road rage. That would be the best news he could give Glenn next to his acquittal. But the sun was so bright that it created a glare and made it impossible to see who was inside. The vehicle eased to a stop in front of the bodega.

Just then, a customer emerged from the bodega and he hurried along and watched his feet. He stepped off the sidewalk and Chico stepped in front of him, blocking his path.

The man raised his hands in surrender to Chico and tried to step around him. Chico moved with him and shoved him to the ground. He stood over the man and searched every pocket. Removing his wallet from his pants, he took out the money and tossed the wallet at his feet.

"I've seen enough," Buckley said, and pressed the button on the walkie-talkie. "Let's move in and take these guys down!"

"On the count of murder one, we, the jury, find the defendant, Glenn Bebout . . ."

BUCKLEY STOMPED ON the brakes and his Crown Victoria skidded towards the sidewalk, stopping less than a foot away from the curb.

Members of the gang quickly scattered and two-dozen officers dressed in S.W.A.T. uniforms swarmed in on their location from five different directions.

"Get down on the ground!" an officer shouted and the other officers also screamed their commands, creating a chorus of authority and demanded compliance.

The police officers advanced forward methodically, holding their weapons tight against their shoulders and their eyes looking down the sights of their guns.

Several members of the gang dropped to their knees and raised their hands over their heads. But Chico and Paco started to run. Buckley was out of his car and started to chase them. He caught up to Chico and reached out and grabbed his arm. A fellow officer jumped on top of Paco and Buckley tackled Chico to the ground.

Hitting the pavement chin first, Chico moaned out in pain. Momentum kept Buckley moving forward and he leapt into the air and drove a knee into the small of Chico's back.

"I ain't an old lady you can intimidate!" Buckley breathed into Chico's mangled ear hole, his words filled with distaste. He ground his knees into Chico's back. "You're a lowlife!"

Chico flailed and wheezed as he struggled to draw a breath.

"Stop resisting and give me your hands," Buckley said, and grabbed Chico's right forearm and twisted his arm behind his back. He pushed a cuff onto his wrist and made it as tight as he could.

"I'm not resisting," Chico said, barely able to speak.

"I said to stop resisting," Buckley shouted at him and pressed his weight on him even more. Buckley took control of his left wrist and wrenched it behind his back and pushed it up towards his head.

Chico kicked in pain. "Alright. You're going to break my damn arm!"

"Believe me, I'd like to do more than that," Buckley said, and secured his other wrist in the cuff.

"You don't seem tough or scary to me. You're just a punk."

"You say that with all of your friends around."

Buckley grabbed the chain in between the cuffs and twisted it. "I could ask them to leave and I could take those cuffs off if you're feeling brave."

LINDA HELD THE microphone firmly. "I've just gotten word that Officer Bebout has been acquitted of murder one."

The crowd of people reacted to the ruling with applause and shouts of delight. The camera focused on a woman that fell to her knees and lifted her arms up in victory. "Finally, justice has been served!"

"As you can see," Linda said and the camera slowly panned back to her, "the support for the Bebout family is overwhelming and there is already a great sense of relief that has replaced the nervous tension. And although what I'm about to say is not yet confirmed, I've gotten word that Officer Bebout might make a statement from the courthouse steps. We will wait here until we can confirm whether or not that rumor is true."

chapter 21

A MAKESHIFT STAGE, complete with a podium and speaker system was quickly constructed after the announcement of Officer Glenn Bebout's acquittal. He requested time to make a public statement and news spread quickly as an already large crowd continued to grow. There were several hundred people gathered, and at the podium, a bouquet of microphones awaited Glenn's arrival.

When Glenn's defense team emerged from the courthouse, the crowd erupted with applause and began to chant, "Bebout is out!"

Glenn and Stefanie emerged only moments later, holding hands and the crowd's energy built to a roar.

Stefanie was crying and Glenn helped usher her along, placing her beside him at the podium. Glenn adjusted one of the microphones and withdrew a written statement from his pocket as the crowd hushed to a complete silence.

"From the bottom of my heart," Glenn's voice echoed, "thank you all for your support through this very trying time."

The microphone squealed and the crowd broke out into a frenzied cheer. Like a trained politician, Glenn lifted his hands and brought an immediate calm to the crowd.

"I thank you for all your letters, phone calls, and gifts of support. You all have made an insufferable time reasonably bearable and I can't express enough thanks for that. With the support of my wife, I am planning on addressing the very difficult task of caring for my brother and raising his twin girls. My focus is on rebuilding our lives and to try and leave the past behind us. And although I am happy and grateful with the outcome of the trial, I am troubled by the series of events that have plagued my family since the night of the tragic accident that left my brother paralyzed. This is why I've asked to speak to you all today."

Glenn wiped the beads of sweat off of his brow and he licked his dry lips.

"You can really get to know yourself when you spend most of your day in a small cell. I spent much of that time thinking about Brick's parents and friends and what they had to endure because of my actions."

The crowd objected to the mention of Brick's name with a boo. Glenn lifted hands, asking for silence and the crowd complied.

"I understand the expectation of your continued anger as well as my own, but that will not console my wife, care for my brother, or nurture his children. Everyone needs to put some stability back into their lives. It is time to start healing."

The crowd to Glenn's left shifted and swayed and a rumble of displeased voices interrupted Glenn's thought. A large guy pushed his way towards the podium.

"Is that how this is going to be?" the man shouted back at the crowd, and turned a baleful eye towards Glenn.

Glenn matched his gaze. He came in contact with guys like this all the time on the job, and this moment was no different. He knew if he showed any fear that would only embolden this guy.

"He said he thought about Brick's parents and how they might have felt," the man in the crowd said. "Some detective he is!" He laughed and pointed. "They've both been dead for years! If anyone here really cares, my name is Macho and I'm Brick's brother. I'm the only family he has left and I assure you that none of you can imagine the pain I'm feeling. All of you celebrate the man that is responsible for killing him in cold blood and you think we're the monsters?"

He quickly turned around and pointed at Glenn.

"That man right there, he's the monster! He premeditated my brother's death and he's free to walk! Tell me, where is the justice in that?"

Macho spat at Glenn. "You're a bastard!" he said, and reached inside his jacket and pulled out a piece of brick and hurled it at Glenn.

Glenn dropped to the ground and pulled Stefanie down with him. He pushed her behind the cover of the podium and watched his attacker wind up with a second piece of brick and hurl it. The first piece skipped past them only a few feet away and Stefanie pulled her knees to her chest and covered her head with her hands. Glenn lay on top of her and tried covering her as best he could.

The second piece pounded off the podium and took a dangerous bounce off the ground that found its way to one of the attorneys that shouted out in pain. Glenn looked to see what the damage was and another full-sized brick hit the cement a few feet away from him. The brick fragments that chipped away sprayed Glenn, stinging his skin.

Members of the crowd along with court officer's wrestled Macho down, and they took away the last brick he attempted to hurl.

"I wish I could cause you the same pain you caused me," Macho shouted, ripe with anger.

His focus was locked on Glenn and his eyes were wide. The strain of his shouting made the veins in his neck bulge. "You killed my brother, you son of a bitch! You killed him and I will not rest until you pay!"

THE QUIET FIGURE that had a shawl covering its head watched the man approach the podium, shout his protest, and begin heaving bricks in a desperate attempt to seek revenge without having to serve a lot of time for it.

It was the perfect opportunity to make a move while everyone was distracted.

Pulling the shawl a bit lower so that it covered the face, the figure continued to weave through the crowd delicately as not to draw any attention.

Settling about five rows back on the opposite side of the man that yelled while he was being restrained a certain calmness took over. For the moment, it was important to remain ordinary so that when the crowd reorganized, they would provide the cover needed to get close enough.

STEFANIE PULLED HER knees to her chest and covered her head with her hands to try and shield herself from the man that started shouting and hurling bricks. These people were crazy, and the feeling of panic took her back to the moment the hunk of cement came crashing through her bedroom window and landed on her bed with a heavy thump. Tears of helpless frustration and terror consumed her and she wondered if this madness would ever end.

"Be strong," Glenn said from beside her and even made it his business to smile at her. A brick banged off the podium and Stefanie screamed. She scooted over in an attempt to make a run for it.

"No," Glenn said and clamped down on her wrist and held her in place. "Stay where you are. I don't want anything happening to you. You're safe here."

"No, I'm not," Stefanie said and pulled away.

"Yes, you are," Glenn said, and he lay on top of her.

She instantly felt safe in his protective care and was reminded how she wanted that when the people were outside their bedroom window, taunting her.

"We're fine," Glenn said. "There are plenty of cops here. They won't let anything happen to us."

As suddenly as it began, the attack ended. "You see?" Glenn said, and rolled off her.

Stefanie dared to look around the side of the podium and she saw the guy was kicking and screaming below a pile of bodies that wrestled him into submission.

A hand was held out in front of Stefanie's face and her eyes slowly moved up the arm and to Glenn's face.

"Come, let's get you off of the ground," he said.

She placed her hand into his and was gently pulled to her feet. She hugged him tight and didn't want to ever let him go.

"Now let's finish this and go home," Glenn said and kissed the side of her face and stepped back to the podium.

"I know the hurt and anger these events have created a division in this community. You've seen it here, just now, and it is ugly," Glenn said.

He drew the attention of the crowd and the police took Macho away.

Stefanie stared at Glenn, no longer hearing his words. She could only see his strength and knew she would be safe from everything that plagued them.

"It's important we begin the healing process and let go of our anger. As a community we can begin to do that. We can make this a safe place to live again."

The crowd applauded his words.

THE PERSON THAT was shrouded with the shawl emerged into the front row, simple, discreet and watching Glenn with disdain. He was an arrogant man and was deserving of what was coming to him. He stood behind the podium and spoke of apologies that meant nothing and wallowed about the misfortunes that life can hand you in an attempt to gain the crowd's sympathy. It was pathetic, insulting and provoking.

And now the time had finally come to act and to do so swiftly.

Leaping onto the makeshift stage, a gun was pulled out of the waistband and before anyone even realized what was happening, Glenn was standing less than five feet away, looking down the barrel of a gun.

Aiming the gun at the center of his chest, the shrouded person flipped the shawl off of her head, and shouted, "Do you think you can get away with what you've done?"

The crowd shrieked and those nearest Glenn scrambled for cover. She trained the gun on Glenn's chest. "Tell your cop friends to stay where they are," Ruth said. "There are plenty of us here, hidden within the crowd. We'll massacre everyone if anyone tries to be a hero."

Glenn raised his hands in surrender. "I am unarmed."

"I'm not."

"Let my wife go. She has nothing to do with this."

"She has everything to do with this. She stays," Ruth said, and Stefanie remained unmoving. "I want her to watch you die. That is so important to keeping the cycle of dysfunction alive. Look at all of these people I get to shock today."

"No one else has to die," Glenn said.

Ruth laughed. "Oh yes, someone does," she said and moved the gun between Glenn's head and chest. "But the sad part is that you don't even know who I am, do you?"

"A Sinner," Glenn said.

Ruth smiled. "Yes, a Sinner like you. Thou shalt not kill."

"I don't even remember doing it."

"So that justifies his death?"

"No, it doesn't."

"I knew we could find a way to agree."

"Please, take me and leave these people alone. I'll go with you willingly."

"There's nowhere for you to go."

The stalemate made Glenn groan.

"I know it's probably horrible not having control," Ruth said. "How long have you been hiding behind the power of your badge and the success of your brother?"

"I don't hide. I'm right here, and I want to know what I can do to make this go away?"

"Go away?" she laughed. "Your death. But first I want you to ask me my name."

Glenn didn't respond.

"Ask me my name!" she shouted, insane.

He flinched. "What is your name?"

"My name is Ruth."

"It's nice to meet you Ruth."

"Is it really?" She looked at the gun she held. "I couldn't imagine this helping you in coming to that decision."

"It doesn't have to be like this."

"Yes, it does," she said and paused. "I'm Brick and Macho's half sister. I just got them back and your family is responsible for taking them away from me."

Glenn stared.

"Move close to him," Ruth said to Stefanie and motioned with the gun. "I want you to get a good look at him before I kill him."

Stefanie stood close to Glenn and tears streamed down her face.

"So you're the wife of the bastard brother?"

"I am his wife, yes," Stefanie said.

"Do you love him?"

Stefanie began to bawl uncontrollably. "More than anything and I wish I could have given him the child he always wanted."

"I loved the man your husband gunned down inside this courthouse. He was my brother and he always tried to protect me against people like your husband. Now I'll never get to hear the sound of his voice ever again."

"I'm sorry for that," Stefanie said.

"Are you?" Ruth said. "And what about all of these people that have come to praise your husband? Do you think they suddenly believe my brother's life was worth a damn?"

Stefanie stared for a moment. "I don't know."

"No, they don't," Ruth said and lowered the gun. She heaved a sigh and looked at Glenn. "You killed my brother!" She raised the gun, took aim, and squeezed the trigger.

To her delight, Glenn fell in a heap and everyone began to scream.

"You see?" she shouted. "No one will ever be the same again!"

STEFANIE FELL TO her knees and pulled Glenn's limp body onto her lap. She ran her fingers through his blood-soaked hair and unknowingly smeared brain matter.

"It's going to be okay, help is coming."

He gurgled on blood that filled his mouth and his body convulsed.

RUTH QUICKLY TURNED and pointed her gun at a large man that charged up the courthouse steps. Two flashes that came from the big man's side and the immediate meaty slap of something hitting her stomach made her pause.

Her belly was on fire, and strangely, it reminded her of the burning ash end of her cigarette that had dropped on her thigh and distracted her while she was driving. But this was much more painful and it dwelled deep inside.

All of her strength drained out of her body and she was unable to handle the weight of the gun. Lowering the weapon, she fell to her knees and looked at her stomach. A steady flow of blood brought a smile to her face. She fell forward and as she struggled to get a breath, she watched Stefanie comforting Glenn in his last moments.

"I got you back, you bastard. You killed my brother."

She tasted blood and tried to spit it out but her tongue felt swollen and tasted like tin. A consuming darkness descended upon her and she succumbed to its call.

BUCKLEY PULLED INTO the packed parking lot of the courthouse and couldn't believe the amount of people that gathered to rally in support of Glenn. There were hundreds of people and dozens of news reporters. The verdict had been announced over the radio and he couldn't wait to give Glenn a hug. He wanted to tell him about the arrests he made and how the Sinners were fragmented and on the run.

Sudden chaos filled the crowd and people were scrambling in a desperate attempt to find cover. Distant screams of terror drew him out of his vehicle and at a full run across the parking lot. A shortness of breath demanded he stop but an absolute need to get to Glenn compelled him to draw his weapon and keep moving.

Bouncing off of a woman and knocking her to the ground, Buckley didn't break stride. Every second counted and he knew it.

Approaching the makeshift podium, Buckley saw an unidentified woman that stood over Glenn. At a glance, he saw Glenn on the ground and Stefanie kneeling beside him.

The woman's eyes opened wide and she turned towards him. Forced to take aim and fire his weapon in mid stride, he tapped the trigger twice and the woman froze, seeming stunned.

He watched her fall to her knees and she no longer mattered. Glenn was bleeding from his head and Stefanie clung to him. She was covered in his blood and she rocked him back and forth, speaking to him gently.

Buckley dropped to his knees and looked at his dead friend, and shouted, "No! Not him too!"

chapter 22

BUCKLEY SAT IN the center seat of his leather sofa and had his feet on the coffee table. He had a tall glass of water in his hand and the remote control for the television in the other.

"The kids are going to be staying at her mother's house for the next several days," he said to his wife Jackie. She sat next to him, curled up and in her nightgown.

"She needs time to grieve," Jackie said. "I'm glad she agreed to stay here for a few days."

"Me too," he said, and nodded at the bathroom door. "She's been in there a long time. Do you think she's okay?"

"She has a lot to process. If she's not out in five minutes, I'll check on her."

"Okay," he said, and satisfied with that, he raised the volume on the television. News reporter Linda Lou was at the courthouse. High barricades had been erected and blocked the view of the makeshift podium where Glenn had been shot. The streets were littered with debris and the area was strangely vacant.

"Merely twenty four hours ago, this location was like something out of the Wild West," Linda Lou said.

Clips of the chaos that consumed the courthouse steps began to play. A still frame of Ruth aiming her gun at Glenn faded into a distant shot of a bloody Glenn lying on the ground with Stefanie cradling him in her lap.

"Shootouts," Linda said.

A photo of Ruth aiming her weapon at Buckley appeared.

"Lives and a community forever changed."

A new photo of Ruth lying on the ground dead, and Buckley kneeling beside Glenn and Stefanie, crying out in anguish, gave him the chills.

A lump formed in the middle of his throat and he tried to wash it down with a giant gulp of water.

"Turn this off," Jackie said. "She doesn't need to be hearing or seeing anything like this."

A sharp knock at the front door prompted him to look at the clock on the cable box.

"It's nine fifteen. You've got to be kidding me," he muttered and shut the television off. "You're right, just like she doesn't need these hounds harassing her either."

He stood, pulled up his pants and walked to the front door. Opening it with anger, he said, "I've already told you guys we're not making any statements."

A young man with long hair that wore a black leather jacket had a gun pointed between Buckley's eyes. "Hello, hero."

Buckley turned to see where his gun was.

"Ah, I wouldn't do that," the man at the door said.

The gun was on the end table opposite his wife.

"The things you've done sicken me. You shot my girlfriend and she was the only person in the world I ever loved."

"She was a thug and so are you," Buckley said.

"And I'm the worst kind there is," he said.

BETO LOOKED DOWN the street both ways one last time. It had been about an hour since his target last had a visitor.

He knocked on the door, drew his weapon and took aim.

Although he had a falling out with Brick, it was over an untruth. His love for Ruth was more valuable to him than the gang or the breaking of the bond of siblings. When he made the oath to always look out for one another, he meant it.

The door swung open and the fat guy looked at him.

"I've already told you guys we're not making any statements."

"Hello, hero," Beto said.

The fat man's fear was palpable and when he turned to have a look inside his house, Beto tightened his grip on the gun. "Ah, I wouldn't do that."

The fat man looked back at him with anger.

"The things you've done sicken me. You shot my girlfriend and she was the only person in the world I ever loved."

"She was a thug and so are you!"

His words were infuriating but Beto didn't want to show he wasn't in control. "And I'm the worst kind there is," he said, and squeezed the trigger.

Blam!

The gun exploded with power. It kicked back in his hands and his face was sprayed with blood. The large man dropped to the floor with a heavy thump. The woman inside the house started to scream and he took aim and finished her off with two quick rounds.

He spit on Buckley and tucked the gun in his waistband. Covering it with his shirt, he turned around and walked away, his focus on rebuilding the gang.

STEFANIE LOOKED IN the mirror and dabbed her swollen, red eyes with a tissue. She was tired from crying and her heart hurt something fierce. The pain felt eternal and the question of what she was supposed to do now that she was a widow haunted her. She had to care for her brother-in-law that was in a vegetative state and his two children.

"Get yourself together," she said at her reflection. "I'm not going to allow myself to get pulled into that deep dark hole that swallowed Jennifer up. I can't. I have people that are depending on me."

Pow!

She froze, recognizing the sound of gunfire and heard Jackie scream.

Pow! Pow!

Opening the bathroom door, she spied the living room and saw a man at the door walking away. Jackie's head was bleeding and she was slumped over, unmoving.

Her first instinct was to call out to Buckley, but she slapped her hand over her mouth and stifled any sound. She didn't want to draw the attention of the person that left.

Exiting the bathroom, she immediately spotted Buckley face down with a massive amount of blood pooling around his head.

She hurried to the gun on the end table, grabbed it, and ran out the door. Seeing the man walking down the street, she immediately pursued him with haste and an equal amount of caution.

When she caught up to him, she took aim at his head and spoke through clenched teeth. "You!" she said, and he faced her. "I've had enough!"

Click!

The gun didn't fire.

"I WANT YOU to feel safe while you are here," Buckley said to Stefanie. She was sitting on the right side of the sofa and Jackie was on the left side, leaving the center seat unoccupied.

He walked behind the couch and placed his gun on the end table next to Stefanie and gave it a pat.

"It's there if you need it," he said, and walked around the couch and sat between the ladies. "It has never let me down."

"Thank you," Stefanie said. "I appreciate both of you looking after me."

"You can stay as long as you'd like," Jackie said, and Buckley nodded.

Stefanie smiled. "Excuse me, I need to use the restroom."

Buckley watched her walk to the bathroom and gently close the door and lock it.

"I don't think you should have given her a gun," Jackie said.

"I'm just trying to make sure she feels safe," he said.

"She's safe by us being here for her. That's all she needs right now."

"It's piece of mind," he said. "But don't worry about it, it's not loaded and it's not like she's really going to need it."

He took his drink, put his feet on the table and grabbed the television remote.

about the author

KEITH ROMMEL is a self taught award-winning author and screen-writer. Writing in an array of different genres, Keith Rommel's work has been called "Horror for the curious mind" and "Thinking man's fiction." He lives in Florida with a ghost that keeps him company late into the night.